One Step
to
Paradise

Books by Jasmine Cresswell

Knave of Hearts
For Love of Christy
One Step to Paradise
Master Touch
Dear Adam
Under Cover of Night
Surprised by Love
Refuge in His Arms
Imprisoned Heart
Tender Triumph
Runaway Love
Stormy Reunion

One Step
to
Paradise

Jasmine Cresswell

SPEAKING VOLUMES, LLC

NAPLES, FLORIDA

2012

One Step to Paradise

ISBN 978-1-61232-815-7

Chapter One

THE WOMAN SEATED next to Dan Matthews on the plane was petite, raven-haired, and beautiful, and she didn't hesitate to let him know she was also one-hundred percent available. She told him her name and half her life history before the stewardess finished serving breakfast, and by the time the plane was ready to land at Stapleton Airport she had already given him her address and phone number, along with detailed directions for driving to her apartment.

Just for a moment Dan thought longingly about cool sheets and hot, entwined bodies. Since his divorce five years earlier, he had worked hard at keeping his sexual relationships free of emotional involvement, and he recognized instantly that this particular woman was playing right in his league. He experienced a definite twinge of regret when he told her that his schedule in Denver was too full to allow any time for rest and recreation, tempting though she made the prospect seem.

He collected his garment bag from the stewardess, reflecting wryly that these days his schedule always seemed too full. It must be at least two months since he'd last taken a woman to bed, and far longer than he cared to remember since he'd been interested enough in one to put himself through the hassle of calling for a date.

This, however, was not the moment to start philosophizing about the inadequacies of his sex life. He walked quickly out of the arrivals lounge, passing through the main concourse and out into the blazing Colorado sunshine. He hailed a passing taxi with a brisk, efficient snap of his fingers.

"Cherry Hills, please," he said to the driver. "Four Rocky Canyon Lane. It's just north of Quincy and east of University."

The cabdriver grunted, and Dan settled back into the torn leather passenger seat, glancing toward the Rocky Mountain foothills as the driver headed west out of the airport. It was mid-June, but he could still see snow on a couple of the more distant peaks. He shut his eyes, suddenly aware that he was hovering dangerously close to exhaustion.

The last month had been even more stress filled than usual. A week ago Dan had been in China. Three days ago he'd been negotiating the final stages of a joint manufacturing agreement in Singapore. This morning he had left his apartment in Connecticut at six in order to make the eight o'clock flight out of La Guardia to Denver.

All this frantic flying, Dan thought ruefully, just because Charlie Steddon had been too damned infatuated to realize when he was being fleeced by a first-rate con artist. All this, because some blonde bombshell with huge breasts and miniscule morals had somehow persuaded the street-wise Charlie to rewrite his will.

Dan's mouth hardened into a tight, straight line. He had been in Hong Kong when word of Charlie's death reached him last month. Charlie had lived sixty-six hard-drinking, heavy-smoking years, but Dan still hadn't been prepared for the news. Charlie was not only Dan's uncle by marriage, he had also been his business partner and

friend. Or at least Dan had thought they were friends—
until his last conversation with the company lawyer, Frank
Goldberg. Now, however, he was beginning to wonder.

A tropical storm off the coast of Hong Kong had
prevented Dan from flying home in time for his uncle's
funeral, so he hadn't yet had the pleasure of telling the
former Mrs. Charlie Steddon precisely what he thought
of her. The anticipation of that upcoming confrontation
was the one ray of sunlight in the otherwise bleak land-
scape ahead of him.

It galled Dan no end to know he was going to have
to buy off Charlie's scheming widow, but Frank had made
it clear he had no other choice. Dan had already given
away one fortune to his ex-wife. It was infuriating to
realize he would have to hand over another in order to
take care of Charlie's inexplicable obsession with a woman
young enough to be his granddaughter.

The cab drew up in the circular driveway of a huge
house, whose architect had apparently suffered from the
delusion that he was designing a medieval German castle.
A giant television antenna sprouted incongruously from
behind one turreted corner of the roof, and an elaborate
sprinkler system was methodically protecting lush beds
of pink and red geraniums from Denver's arid, desertlike
air. Even from inside the taxi Dan could see that the
massive, iron-studded front door was wired to a complex
system of spotlights and electronic burglar alarms. Ev-
idently Charlie's widow liked her historic splendor lib-
erally modified by modern-day conveniences.

The cabbie spoke without turning around. "This is it,
buddy. Number four, Rocky Canyon Lane."

"Thanks." Dan paid off the driver and looked around
with interest as he walked across the flagstoned courtyard. Charlie had kept a small apartment in Manhattan,

which was where the two men had usually met to discuss company business. Dan had never visited his partner's home in Colorado and had never been introduced to Charlie's wife.

Dan had a clear mental image of her, however, thanks to his mother, who had flown out to Denver immediately after hearing the stunning news of her brother-in-law's marriage. Unfortunately, Mrs. Matthew's visit had not been a success, and in seven years it had never been repeated.

Charlie had never told his sister-in-law where he'd met Corinne, his new wife, nor had he done much to explain his decision to marry again after years of comfortable widowhood. But after one look at Corinne, Mrs. Matthews scarcely needed any explanations. Charlie had obviously succumbed to some form of early senility, despite his apparently sharp wits.

The new Mrs. Steddon was a total disaster, as far as Martha Matthews was concerned. She was tall, with a large bust and rounded hips that she encased in tight T-shirts and even tighter jeans. She had dark blue eyes and hair so startlingly blonde that Dan's mother could tell at a glance that the color owed everything to a bottle and nothing at all to nature. During the three days of Mrs. Matthew's visit, Corinne's face was always thick with makeup, no doubt applied in the hope of disguising the scheming cast of her features. But of course, Martha Matthews had reported angrily, no paint could hide the fact that Corinne was a conniving hussy and slightly harder than reinforced concrete.

Corinne's worst offense—at least according to Mrs. Matthews—was that she made no effort whatsoever to disguise the fact that she was forty years younger than her husband. Dan, more realistic than his mother, wondered exactly how even the most well-meaning nineteen-year-old could set about making herself look like a suitable wife for a crusty fifty-nine year old widower.

Once he got over his initial amazement at his uncle's marriage, Dan had refused to let thoughts of Charlie's teenage bride interfere with the excellent relationship the two men had always enjoyed. He achieved his goal by simply pretending that Corinne didn't exist. Dan had gone through college at the end of the turbulent sixties, and he liked to think of himself as a free-spirited liberal, especially when it came to other people's sexual habits. Corinne, however, was more than he could stomach. Nineteen-year-old girls who married men forty years their senior were obviously looking for one thing only—and he was quite sure it wasn't companionship.

Impatiently, Dan pushed his reflections aside. He lifted the lion's-head knocker and banged loudly on the iron-studded door. Corinne would be twenty-six by now, he thought. Twenty-six and the possessor of Charlie's whole personal fortune, along with a fifty-one percent interest in the Dansted Corporation, Charlie and Dan's plumbing-supplies company. Not a bad return on a seven-year investment, he reflected cynically.

Even now, Dan couldn't quite believe what Charlie had done to him. The Dansted Corporation had been a true partnership, with Charlie providing most of the original capital and Dan contributing his technical knowledge and financial flair. Although he'd had two weeks to get used to the idea, Dan still had trouble accepting what the company lawyer had told him. Dan had picked up the phone in his Connecticut apartment, never dreaming of the shock in store for him.

"Dan, I think you should know that we had a call

from Corinne yesterday," Frank Goldberg had said.

"Corinne?" Dan had been packing for his trip to China, and was busy stashing toiletries into his travel bag. He'd been so successful in blocking out thoughts of his uncle's marriage that for a split second the name didn't register.

"Yes. Corinne Steddon, Charlie's widow. Like I said, she called yesterday and insisted on speaking to me personally. The thing is, she claimed to have another will in her possession, more recent than the one in our files. She sent me a copy by express mail, and it arrived this morning. I've looked it over, Dan, and it seems perfectly in order to me."

"What are you trying to tell me, Frank?"

"In this new will, Charlie's left all his Dansted stock to Corinne. He's left it outright, unless she marries again. No strings as long as she stays single."

There was a short silence. "Charlie owned fifty-one percent of the stock," Dan said slowly. "In his old will, he left that in trust for Corinne, with me as executor. He had to write his will that way, otherwise I wouldn't be in control of the voting rights."

"Dan, I drew up that original will for Charlie. I know what it says and why we wrote it as we did."

"Then what the hell happened? Why did Charlie do this to me?"

"I have no idea. He didn't consult me. This will of Corinne's was drawn up by some law firm in Denver. Hudgins and Hoskins. They're perfectly reputable—I've already checked them out." Frank cleared his throat uncomfortably. "As I said, as long as she stays single, Mrs. Steddon retains control of the shares. However, the will stipulates that if she marries, she's obligated to offer the shares to you in exchange for a million dollars, which is the sum Charlie originally invested in the company."

Dan was almost too stunned to feel angry. "Is this crazy will going to make it through the probate courts?" he asked curtly.

Frank hesitated, sounding lawyerlike and cautious even over the phone. "As of this moment, Dan, I'd have to say yes. It's clearly a more recent will than the one in our possession, and none of the clauses is unreasonable—at least in a legal sense."

"In which case, Corinne Steddon owns fifty-one percent of the shares in my company." Dan sat down on the bed. "What exactly does that mean, Frank? Don't give me your usual lawyer talk. I want to know the bottom line—and I'd like it in three sentences or less."

"It means you'd better pray she gets married again, and the sooner the better. Other than that, it means Corinne's the senior partner in the company, and you'll have to get her approval for every expenditure over five thousand dollars. It means you can't negotiate any major contracts without her express written permission. It means she's entitled to consultation about every 'significant' decision. Those were all clauses written into your original agreement with Charlie, and those rights now automatically pass to his beneficiary." Frank paused again. "Mrs. Steddon indicated to me that she wants to discuss the direction of the company's overseas investments with you as soon as possible. She said to let you know she has several interesting suggestions to make about Dansted's future expansion. Apparently she feels it's past time the company started operations in Mexico."

"Started operations in Mexico! Where on earth did she dredge up that particular piece of wisdom? Hell, Frank, from things my mother has told me, I'd say it's a fair guess that Corinne Steddon has entertained herself for the past seven years by painting her toenails, visiting health spas, and spending Charlie's money. Not necessarily in that order. Why would a woman like that want to involve herself in the day-to-day running of a plumbing-supplies company?"

"Who knows? Maybe she's tired of painting her toenails and wants to play at something more interesting."

Dan's voice became very dry. "My most recent deal involved an agreement to export prefabricated bath-drain piping to Hong Kong, and the most exciting part of the transaction was when one of the building inspectors dropped his pen and squirted ink all over the contracts. Once Mrs. Steddon understands what the Dansted Corporation actually does, I can't imagine she'll want anything to do with it."

"Maybe not. But after thirty years as a lawyer, I've given up trying to figure out what people might or might not want to do. Who knows, maybe plumbing hardware turns her on. What I can tell you for sure is that you'd better get your tail out to Denver on the next available plane. And you'd better hope that she's either planning to get married real soon, or is willing to be bought out for a reasonable sum."

Dan's voice became even drier. "Which course of action are you recommending, Frank?"

"Unless you know of some available bachelor looking to change his status, I'm recommending that you buy her out just as soon as you can get your hands on the necessary money. Dansted Corporation can't afford to employ Corinne Steddon. This is a girl who was married at nineteen and hasn't spent a day in gainful employment outside the home since then. If she insists on exercising her right to vote, she could probably run the company into the ground within six months—and that's without even trying. Remember, until you buy her out, she's the majority shareholder. Any time you two disagree, her opinion will be the one that counts."

"Hell, Frank, I can't go out to Denver now! I'm supposed to be flying to China! If you'd called fifteen minutes later, I'd have been on my way to the airport. It took me thirteen weeks to get permission to visit Shanghai, and I have a dozen Chinese government officials lined up, waiting to meet me. I've got to keep my appointments, Frank. Not only is the company's reputation on the line, but hundreds of Chinese villages aren't going to get new piped water supplies unless these agreements are signed."

"Fine. Go to China. God forbid I should be responsible for depriving the Chinese peasants of indoor plumbing. But in the meantime, I'm going to call Corinne Steddon and tell her you'll be coming to see her two weeks from today. And while you're gone, I'll have the accountants draw up an estimate of a fair and reasonable offer for those shares."

Dan returned from his Far Eastern trip to discover that the accountants had come up with the "fair and reasonable estimate" of $3 million for the purchase of Corinne Steddon's shares. Fair and reasonable, Dan concluded grimly, depended very much on who was paying and who was being paid.

Since Dan had nothing like $3 million in liquid assets, it meant he would be forced to borrow $2.75 million from his friendly neighborhood bankers. And since his neighborhood bankers weren't all that friendly when it came to unsecured loans, he soon found out that he would have to mortgage every asset he possessed in order to come up with the necessary collateral. With luck, he supposed he might emerge from the deal still owning his Mazda RX–7, but right now the prospects for retaining outright ownership even of his bicycle were looking distinctly shaky. What the hell! He was always too busy to ride his bicycle anyway.

Corinne Steddon's door was opened at last by an elderly woman wearing a blue coverall. "I'm Daniel Matthews," he said politely. "I have an appointment to see Mrs. Steddon."

The woman didn't smile when she looked at him. "Come in, please. Mrs. Steddon is expecting you."

He followed the maid into a vast living room, which had a marble floor and soaring cathedral ceiling. Sunlight filtering through the lead-pane windows cast odd, rather attractive splashes of color onto the white walls and highlighted the figure of a woman standing in front of a carved oak fireplace.

She was tall and slender, wearing a simple navy-blue linen sheath and plain high-heeled pumps. Her ash-blonde hair was pulled back into a smooth French plait, revealing a face that was pale and perhaps a bit too thin, but of classically beautiful proportions. She wore no jewelry other than a slim gold watch and a pair of plain pearl earrings.

Her appearance was so far removed from his preconceived image of Charlie's widow that Dan gazed quickly around the room, half-expecting some other woman to appear from a dark corner and announce that she was Corinne Steddon.

The maid broke the lengthening silence. "This is Mr. Daniel Matthews, Mrs. Steddon."

"Thank you, Rosita. Would you let us know when you're ready to serve lunch? Mr. Matthews's plane left New York early this morning, and I'm sure he must be hungry."

"It'll be ready at noon. Is that okay?"

Corinne looked at him enquiringly. "Mr. Matthews?"

"Noon would be fine," Dan said. "Whatever's convenient for you and Rosita."

The maid left the room and Corinne walked forward, holding out her hand. "How are you, Mr. Matthews? It's good to meet you at last. Charlie spoke about you often."

He shook her hand. Her fingers felt long and delicate and cool, which made him wonder about the spark of heat he felt at her touch. She removed her hand from his clasp, then looked at him directly for the first time since he'd entered the room. He saw that at least one part of his mother's description had been entirely accurate. Corinne had huge, dark blue eyes fringed with impossibly dark lashes. Dan realized he was staring and turned away, swallowing hard.

"Please accept my condolences on your loss, Mrs. Steddon," he said, speaking with extreme formality. Somehow the prospect of losing his temper and telling Charlie's widow off no longer seemed as appealing as it had for the past two weeks. In some obscure way, he felt it would be dangerous to lose control of himself around Corinne Steddon. He cleared his throat awkwardly. "Charlie was a good man and a wonderful friend."

A faint smile touched her mouth. "He was a wonderful husband, too. Understanding. Loving. Generous."

"Yes, my uncle was certainly generous. Some people might say he was generous to a fault. He never knew when he was being taken for a ride." The terms of Charlie's will had hurt Dan badly, and there was no way he could keep the bitterness out of his voice. He wasn't even sure he wanted to try. He was angry that control of the company—*his* company—had been taken away from him, and he didn't care if Corinne Steddon knew it.

Corinne didn't betray her reaction to Dan's words by

so much as a flicker of an eyelash. "That, too," she said quietly. "Would you care for a drink, Mr. Matthews?"

"No, thank you. It's too early in the day for me to start drinking. But please go ahead if you'd like something."

"I rarely drink," she said flatly. "And certainly not at this time of the day. It was good of you to come and see me, Mr. Matthews. I know how busy you are. So busy, in fact, that it's been seven years since you were last in Denver. Charlie missed those fishing weekends you used to share."

He looked up sharply, caught by some subtle undertone in her voice, but her expression remained neutral. If something was bothering her, she obviously had every intention of keeping it to herself.

"I came out here as soon as I could," he said bluntly. "I'm sure you realize that the terms of Charlie's will came as a big surprise to everybody connected with our company."

"I expect they did," she said. "Although perhaps you wouldn't have found the will so surprising if you'd known a little more about Charlie and me. But then you never made the slightest effort to learn anything about my marriage to Charlie, did you?"

"I felt I knew the salient facts," Dan replied curtly.

She turned away, walking to the fireplace and staring down into the empty grate. "Like the fact that I was nineteen and Charlie was fifty-nine on the day we were married? Is that a *salient fact*, Mr. Matthews?"

"You could say that the age difference always struck me as one of the more fundamental realities of your relationship."

"It was," she said softly. "But there were many others that were equally important."

"I'm sure there were." Dan managed to bite back another, more hostile reply. "Well, Mrs. Steddon, they say it's never too late to make up for lost time, so how about filling me in on some of the missing details in the story of your relationship with my uncle?"

"Such as?"

"Such as where you and Charlie met, for example, and what you were doing with your life at the time."

She turned slowly to face him, and he was surprised to detect a faint but unmistakable gleam of amusement in her dark blue eyes. "Charlie came into an all-night bar where I was working as a cocktail waitress. He asked me to move in with him two weeks after we met. Six months later he asked me to marry him, and I accepted." She lifted her chin in a subtle gesture of defiance. "In case you're wondering, yes, I married him for his money, and yes, Charlie knew exactly what I was doing."

The implicit arrogance of her admission lit the final fuse to Dan's frustration. "That's bully for you, Mrs. Steddon," he said sarcastically. "I sure hope Uncle Charlie lived up to every one of your financial expectations."

"Charlie lived up to all my expectations, in every possible way."

Dan pushed aside the too-vivid images that her words conjured up, doggedly forcing his thoughts back onto the subject of the Dansted Corporation shares. "Mrs. Steddon, I understand from Frank Goldberg, who is our company lawyer, that my uncle's most recent will leaves you with a fifty-one percent ownership of the Dansted Corporation shares."

"Yes, that's right. Charlie changed his will a couple of years ago." Corinne paused and Dan had the sudden crazy suspicion that she was deliberately provoking him, and had been ever since he'd walked into the living room. "Charlie decided around that time that you would probably benefit from my input into the company's decision-making process."

"Benefit from *your* input!" Dan exclaimed.

"Charlie had great faith in my abilities, Mr. Matthews, and while he considered your business judgment impeccable, he didn't consider you a very good judge of people. Without him around to advise you, he felt quite certain the Dansted Corporation would need my help."

Dan fought the urge to tell her—at great length and in unflattering detail—precisely how useful a former cocktail waitress was likely to be when it came to such tasks as negotiating a contract for the supply of preformed bath drains to the Hong Kong Department of Municipal Housing. He reminded himself that he never lost his cool during business negotiations and consoled himself with the thought that her statements about Charlie were so preposterous that it would be charitable to ignore them. Good grief, Charlie had known him from the day he was born and had never once suggested that Dan's people-handling skills were in the least inadequate. In fact, the Dansted Corporation had excellent employee relations. They hadn't had a strike in the factory since it started producing ten years ago. Dan fixed his mouth into a tight smile, not caring if Corinne could see more than a touch of patronization in his expression.

"Mrs. Steddon, I don't think this conversation is proving of much benefit to either of us, so I'd like to get right to the point. I'm here today to make you a formal offer for the shares you now own in the Dansted Corporation. Two weeks ago, before I left for China, I asked our auditors to come up with a fair and reasonable offer for your fifty-one percent interest in my company. They suggest that three million dollars would be a generous sum, but I'm more than willing to have investment analysts of your choice go over the books and—"

"Thank you, but there's no need for investment analysts, Mr. Matthews. I have no intention of selling my shares. I'm looking forward to working with you as a full-time, active partner."

Dan reminded himself for the second time in minutes that he was famous for his calm and courtesy during the most difficult negotiations. He drew several deep, calming breaths. "If you're trying to bid up the price, Mrs. Steddon, I'm afraid you're out of luck. My bankers wouldn't float me for more than three million even if I wanted to pay it."

There was a lengthy silence, during which she looked at him with the cool interest usually displayed by research scientists examining a mutant species of insect. "You seem to be having difficulty understanding me, Mr. Matthews. I repeat; I'm not planning to sell my shares, and I think our discussions would be much more productive if you'd accept that simple fact."

"Maybe you've misunderstood what the Dansted Corporation is all about, Mrs. Steddon. It isn't a big, glamorous company, you know. We have a factory employing about a hundred skilled and semi-skilled workers. The corporate offices are located right next door to the plant, and we employ a minimum administrative staff, mostly junior clerks, together with a few engineers who act as salesmen and plant managers. Why in the world would you want to work in a place like that?"

Without replying, she turned to look out one of the mullioned windows, and sunlight profiled the outline of her body beneath the linen dress. Dan couldn't help noticing that there was still one other aspect of his mother's description that had been entirely accurate. Corinne Steddon possessed a pair of *very* generously curved breasts. He realized suddenly just how attractive her body was, the thrust of her firm breasts all the more alluring for being subtly concealed behind the dark fabric and simple style of her dress. His mind wandered off into the sort of erotic fantasy he thought he had left behind in high school, and he had some difficulty forcing it back to the present. He realized belatedly that he'd missed the first part of Corinne's reply.

"... keeping my shares because Charlie asked me to, and I'm planning to work with the company for the same reason. I promised my husband that I would take an active interest in the Dansted Corporation, and I don't intend to break that promise."

"Very well, Mrs. Steddon." Dan's voice was clipped, and he didn't bother to hide his frustration. At this precise moment, he wasn't sure whether he was more angry with Charlie for writing such a ridiculous will, or with Corinne Steddon for refusing to behave reasonably and accept the $3 million she'd been offered. It was bad enough that he'd have to mortgage his soul to buy her off. It was even worse that she was refusing the offer. But he'd be damned if he was going to let her mess up a business it had taken ten years to build.

Finally winning the struggle to bring his temper under control, he spoke without any particular emphasis. "If you won't agree to sell your shares, Mrs. Steddon, the company lawyers have informed me that I have a legal obligation to facilitate your inspection of the company's physical plant and financial records. Charlie and I always used to meet in his Manhattan apartment on the second Friday of the month. If that time and place would be convenient for you next month, I would be willing to—"

"Oh no, Mr. Matthews! I want us to meet much more often than once a month. I really want to feel part of your day-to-day decision-making process. I plan to sell this house and find somewhere to live in Rhode Island, close to the factory. My schedule will be a little hectic for a while, but I should be able to start work about nine o'clock next Monday morning. Could you have some office space available for me by then? And a copy of all the latest financial reports, of course."

Her whole speech was horrifying, but Dan latched on to the part that struck him as most horrific. "Next Monday!" he exclaimed. "You're planning to start work in my company next Monday?"

She smiled sweetly at him. "Isn't that soon enough? Perhaps I could manage Friday of this week if I really pushed my arrangements..."

He gritted his teeth. "Please don't put yourself out on my account, Mrs. Steddon. Next Monday will be quite soon enough."

"That's good." She gave him another sunny smile. "And since we're going to be working so closely together, I think we should dispense with all this old-fashioned formality, don't you? If you'll call me Corinne, I'll call you Dan."

Just then the maid arrived to announce lunch, preventing Dan from saying something he would undoubtedly have regretted later. He followed Corinne into the cavernous dining room and took his place at one end of the enormous, mock-baronial table. He and Corinne would need microphones to hear each other's conversation, he thought gloomily. He wondered how she'd managed to persuade poor old Charlie to go for such absurd and ostentatious displays of wealth. Worse, he wondered what havoc she'd try to wreak on the comfortable, sensible organization of his company. Unless he could persuade her to take the $3 million, the possibilities for disaster seemed virtually endless.

If he couldn't buy her off, perhaps he could get her married. Dan tried hard to think of any bachelor friends who might be interested in a wealthy widow, but unfortunately not a single name sprang to mind. One way and another, he decided, this was proving to be an exceptionally trying day.

Chapter Two

CORINNE WAS SO tense when she pulled into the Dansted Corporation parking lot that she dropped her purse and had to scrabble around to pick up the coins, credit cards, and lipstick tubes that scattered all over the car floor.

She put everything back neatly in her purse, willing herself not to feel hot and flustered, and got out of the car, drawing deep breaths to steady her nerves as she walked toward the office entrance. This was an important moment in her life, and she had to make sure Dan Matthews didn't throw her off stride, as he had so effectively done at their original meeting. For a start, she'd have to forget the fact that her new business partner was one of the best-looking men she'd seen outside the pages of *Gentlemen's Quarterly*. She had known Charlie's death would make a big difference to her sexual awareness, but she hadn't expected the change to occur so soon. She'd been astonished to find that after seven years of effortless celibacy, Dan's strong features, thick brown hair, and intriguing silver-gray eyes had caused a distinctly erotic flutter of her senses. Not to mention the effect on her senses of his sleekly muscled six-foot-two body.

In some ways, she reflected, Dan's good looks were a welcome bonus, but they certainly weren't high on her list of priorities, and she planned to discount them when making her final decision about approaching him with her proposition.

At this moment she needed to do two things, and both of them quickly. First, she had to decide how she could cause Dan a maximum amount of aggravation without actually affecting the profitability of the company's operations. Second, she needed to check out Charlie's statements about the glowing state of his nephew's health. During their brief meeting in Denver, Dan had looked to be in pretty good shape, but Corinne knew all too well that appearances could be deceptive. A few discreet enquiries around the office should give her a more accurate picture of his physical fitness. His IQ, fortunately, wasn't in any doubt. Charlie had boasted constantly about Dan's outstanding college record and his brilliant performance in the graduate program at the Colorado School of Mines.

Corinne pushed at the heavy metal doors and entered a small, high-ceilinged reception area. The sounds of the factory production line were muted to a steady hum in this part of the building, and Corinne guessed that within a day or two she would become so accustomed to the noise that she would no longer hear it. The office décor, however, would take longer to get used to: *army surplus stark* best described it. Shiny green walls and a brown linoleum floor were highlighted in the unflattering glow of fluorescent strip lamps. A display case on the far wall exhibited miscellaneous faucets, drain pipes, and shower heads in long, neat rows. Corinne looked carefully at the display, then decided that however creatively you stacked it, plumbing hardware left much to be desired as a decoration.

A young woman seated behind a gray metal desk was busy answering phone calls. Corinne noticed with a spurt of remembered fellow-feeling that the telephonist's face was covered with angry red pimples. She had tried—not very successfully—to cover the blemishes with a thick, unbecoming layer of makeup.

The receptionist connected another call, then turned to greet Corinne with a warm and friendly smile.

"Can I help you?" she asked cheerfully, pulling a desk calendar toward her. "Do you have an appointment with one of the engineers?"

"No, not specifically. I'm Corinne Steddon. I was planning to start work here this morning."

"You're Mrs. Steddon? But you can't be!" The girl blushed from her neck all the way up to the roots of her lank brown hair. "I'm sorry, I didn't mean that the way it sounded. I—um—I wasn't expecting you to arrive quite so early. Mr. Matthews didn't mention what time you would be coming in. I'm Debbie Jones, Mrs. Steddon, and I'm the receptionist here. I also do some secretarial work for the salesmen if they ever need it."

Debbie's face was scarlet with embarrassment, and Corinne watched her sympathetically. She had long since overcome any sensitivity about the age difference between herself and Charlie, and she understood why the receptionist appeared so shocked. Debbie had obviously known Charlie, who'd looked every one of his sixty-six years, so it wasn't surprising that she'd expected his widow to be at least middle-aged. Corinne could readily forgive Debbie's initial display of shock. But she couldn't forgive Dan; he supposedly loved his uncle dearly, yet in seven years had never bothered to find out the true story behind Charlie's marriage.

However, Dan's character defects were of no particular interest to Corinne, since she belonged to the school of thought that believed character was shaped by environment not hereditary. For her purposes, Dan had only to be intelligent and healthy. She'd take care of the rest. After all, she thought wryly, she herself was living proof that a loving environment could change almost anybody for the better. When Charlie had taken her in, she'd been a hard-mouthed, rebellious high-school dropout, heading straight for disaster. Seven years of his generous loving had transformed her into an entirely different person.

"It's good to meet you, Debbie," she said, deliberately switching her thoughts back to the present. "Has Mr. Matthews arrived yet? I'm anxious to find out what office space he's assigned me. I'm really looking forward to getting started on my new job."

"He came in about a half hour ago, Mrs. Steddon. I'll let him know you've arrived."

"There's no point in bringing him all the way out here just to meet me. Why don't I go directly to his office?"

Debbie gestured toward her headphones. "I'm not supposed to leave the switchboard, Mrs. Steddon, but Mr. Matthew's office is at the end of the corridor. The last door you come to. Would you mind very much going there by yourself?"

"No problem at all." Corinne hoped she sounded more confident than she felt. She gave Debbie a final, brisk smile and set off down the narrow aisle. When she reached the end of the corridor, Corinne tapped lightly on the door.

"Come in."

She walked into the office, subconsciously registering the institutional green paint on the walls, the desk crowded with papers and a slide projector, the rows of steel filing cabinets, and the specially lighted draftsman's desk bearing a half-finished drawing. Her conscious mind registered little more than the fact that there were two men in the room. One, who was short and stocky, she didn't recognize. The other was Dan.

Dan stood by a small window overlooking the company parking lot. He wore the same sort of dark, conservative business suit he'd worn in Denver, but in the privacy of his own office he had discarded the jacket, loosened the tie, and rolled up the shirt-sleeves. He stood with his back toward her, one hand thrust negligently into the pocket of his pants, the other resting on the window ledge. He seemed to be doing nothing more demanding than watching a bakery truck make deliveries at the factory entrance, but Corinne was aware of an almost palpable aura of power and purposefulness surrounding him. Dan Matthews in Denver had been impressive. On his home ground, he was overwhelming.

He turned to greet her, his gray eyes assessing and his smile cool. "Hello, Corinne," he said politely. "It's good to have you here this morning. I hope you didn't have any difficulty finding the plant?"

"None at all, thank you. Your secretary sent me excellent directions. I appreciated her letter." For some crazy reason her heart seemed to be experiencing considerable difficulty in maintaining its usual steady rhythm. Maybe that was why she sounded so abrupt when she said, "As soon as you're ready, I'm looking forward to settling into my office and studying the latest company reports."

Dan's brows rose just a little and his mouth quirked into a small, sardonic smile. "I can see you don't like to waste any time, Corinne. However, I think you should take a few minutes to relax and have a cup of coffee before you plow into twenty-five computerized sheets of production and sales figures."

"Thanks, but I ordered breakfast before I left the motel

this morning, and I'm just about floating away on coffee."

"Then you must meet some of your colleagues and listen to a couple of presentations before we press your nose to the grindstone. For a start, let me introduce you to Warrick Evans; he's our factory manager and the guy who keeps us all from panicking when we're operating behind schedule."

Corinne and Warrick shook hands. "It's a pleasure to meet you," Warrick said, sounding as if he meant it. "I hope you enjoy your day with us, Mrs. Steddon. We don't have a giant operation here yet, but it's efficient and profitable with plenty of room for expansion. Best of all from my point of view, we've won several state awards for our excellent safety record."

"Congratulations," Corinne said. "I'm certainly looking forward to seeing the plant in operation. I noticed in the last report Dan sent my husband that you have a whole new tool-and-die operation starting up. That must make a big difference to your capacity for meeting special orders."

Warrick looked more than a little startled by Corinne's familiarity with the factory plans. "Yes, that's quite true, Mrs. Steddon. In fact, we've found that by—" He seemed to suddenly recollect himself, and shuffled his feet uncomfortably. "Well, we'll talk about that some other time. I have to get back to the factory floor now. I'll be waiting for your call, Dan, whenever Mrs. Steddon is ready to see the plant."

"Thanks. I imagine my presentation will take about an hour, and then Frank wants a word with her. It may be after lunch before we're ready for you." Dan escorted his factory manager out of the office, then shut the door and walked back to the window.

"I thought you might like to see a slide presentation I sometimes make to foreign buyers," he said to Corinne, drawing a pair of thick green drapes across the window. He pulled a viewing screen down from a storage slot built into the ceiling and flipped off the overhead light, leaving the room illuminated only by the dim glow of a special screening lamp. He strolled back to his desk and switched on the slide projector.

"We like to give all our prospective clients an idea of how our company functions; we've found it helps in making sales. I hope these slides will fill you in on some of the background of the Dansted Corporation, and give you some basic ideas about how the company's organized."

"That's very thoughtful of you, Dan," she said, deciding not to mention that she already had a very clear idea of the company's organization. She'd been reading the business reports prepared for Charlie since the earliest days of her marriage.

Five minutes into the presentation, she realized that Dan's intentions had been neither kind nor helpful. Her best guess was that he was trying either to bore her or confuse her into staying away from the company offices. His voice was normally low, authoritative, and pleasant to listen to, but he rambled through the presentation in a flat monotone that was often out of synch with the slides he flashed onto the screen. Anybody who didn't have a fairly accurate idea of what the Dansted Corporation was all about would probably have dozed off in the stuffy darkness.

However, after two years as a high-school dropout, followed by three years as a cocktail waitress, Corinne's tolerance level was high. Having spent the years between fourteen and sixteen with nothing much to do but watch

TV game shows and listen to her parents hurl abuse at each other, it took a lot to bore her.

She sat through the entire presentation without once taking her gaze off the screen. Dan Matthews was obviously bound and determined to be rid of her, she thought, and she was equally bound and determined not to go. She wondered for a moment if he might already be sufficiently desperate to listen to her proposition, but on reflection, she decided that was unlikely. Besides, she hadn't yet had the opportunity to check out his credentials. Before asking somebody to father your prospective child, you needed to make quite certain the candidate was sound of mind and body.

Charlie, of course, had never stopped singing his nephew's praises. According to him, Dan possessed the dynamic combination of Albert Einstein's mental agility and Bruce Jenner's physical prowess. If Dan had any personality failings at all, Charlie blamed them all on his nephew's ex-wife. She had stolen his heart and his money, leaving him hard and calculating in his approach to women. It wasn't that Dan's wife was a bad woman, Charlie had hastened to explain. She and Dan had just been terribly wrong for each other.

Corinne smiled tenderly. Dear Charlie. He'd liked to pretend he was the toughest, roughest guy on the block, but in actual fact his heart had been softer than warm, melted butter. He'd even found something good to say about her father—which, all things considered, was no mean feat.

Dan finally switched off the projector and Corinne rose to her feet, stretching gratefully. She walked over to the window and drew back the drapes before turning to face him head on. Feeling a tiny smile creep across her lips, she admitted to herself that she was rather looking forward to the next few minutes.

"Thank you, Dan," she said with false sweetness. "Thank you for taking so much of your valuable time to fill me in on the operations of the Dansted Corporation. I can see that you've worked hard at the script for that presentation, and the slides are really of a very high standard. Unfortunately, I feel you need a lot of practice before your manner of presentation lives up to the high quality of your material." She smiled with the air of a kindly teacher encouraging a thick-witted student. "After all, Dan, if *you* sound bored, how can you expect your audience to be interested in what you're saying?"

A faint touch of red stained his high cheekbones. "Would you consider that your past experience has qualified you as an expert on business presentations, Corinne?"

"No, I'm not an expert," she said. "But I was voted one of the best in my MBA class at oral presentations, and I have some really helpful tapes that the communications professor used with us during our course. If you'd like, Dan, I would be more than happy to go over those tapes with you and give you some personal coaching sessions. It's amazing how much students can improve with a little private tutoring."

She had to admire the way he controlled the shock that had turned his body momentarily rigid. "You have a Master's degree in business administration? When did you get that?"

The moment was as sweet as she had hoped it would be, and she savored it to the full. "Why, last summer, Dan, didn't you know? I have an undergraduate degree in psychology as well. That was one of the reasons Charlie thought I could be so helpful to the company. Almost all of Dansted's management personnel have engineering backgrounds, so he thought it was time to bring somebody with a different perspective into the company."

Dan walked out from his position behind the desk and stood in front of her. "Why didn't you tell me you had an MBA when I came to see you in Denver?" he asked quietly.

She regarded him steadily. "You never asked. As I recall our meeting, you walked in, expressed disapproval of my marriage to Charlie, and then offered to buy my shares. With those two topics hanging in the air, it didn't seem appropriate to discuss my educational background."

He turned away, crossing the room to disengage the clip holding the screen in place, and spoke without looking at her. "You knew damn well I was deliberately making that presentation boring. Why didn't you stop me?"

"I don't know," she said, surprising herself with the admission. "Maybe I wanted you to realize that I grew up in a hard school, and I can take anything you care to throw at me. Believe me, Dan, sitting in a comfortable chair listening to you make an ass of yourself isn't going to convince me to stay away from the Dansted Corporation."

"You don't have to stay away," he said quietly. "Corinne, I behaved badly when I came to see you in Denver, on both a personal and professional level." He strode restlessly across the small office, and she guessed that his apology was not coming easily. "The honest truth is that I was hurt by the terms of my uncle's will. Charlie provided most of the money that got this company going, but I was the one who turned it from a tiny, backyard operation into a profitable corporation with a flourishing export trade. Ten years ago our total profit for the year was five thousand dollars. This year we've actually made enough money to set up a small experimental design lab.

And that's in addition to paying everybody a productivity bonus."

"Charlie enormously admired what you've done, Dan. You must know that."

"I thought I did, but I'm not so sure anymore. Under the terms of his original will, you retained all your financial benefits as his widow, but I got control of the day-to-day running of the company. That will showed Charlie trusted my business judgment."

"His new will wasn't intended to show any lack of trust."

"Maybe not. But the fact is, Corinne, no company— big or small—can operate efficiently with two presidents. As far as the Dansted Corporation goes, one or the other of us has to have final control."

"Technically, the situation hasn't changed at all since Charlie was alive. After all, he owned the same amount of stock as I now own."

"The technicalities of the situation are irrelevant. Whatever Charlie might have been allowed to do by law, in practice he never questioned my judgments. We had a working relationship that was based on years of mutual respect. But you and I have no past relationship to build on, Corinne, and you've made no secret of the fact that you intend to utilize your majority voting power to overrule me whenever we disagree."

Corinne discovered that her sympathies were very much on Dan's side. From his perspective, even though he'd never made any attempt to gain full possession of the facts, Charlie's will was not entirely fair. She clamped her teeth together just in time to prevent herself from saying that she had no intention of overriding his judgment on any crucial issues, and that as far as she was concerned Dan was still completely in charge of the

Dansted Corporation's major business decisions.

"Well, Dan, we may have to start from scratch, but I'm sure we'll work something out. I'll try not to get under your skin, and I think you'll be surprised at how soon we manage to establish some sort of a decent working relationship." She flashed him another smile. "So, could I please see my office now?"

"Before we go to your office, I'd like to make one final offer for your shares."

"Dan, please don't! I've told you I'm not interested in selling."

"Don't refuse before you've heard what I'm offering. Now that I've had longer to think things over, I can see that my uncle might have been right. You probably have many useful new ideas to contribute to this company, and I shouldn't dismiss them. On the other hand, practical experience counts for a lot in business, Corinne, and I'm the one who has that. What do you say we try to reach some sort of compromise? I'm willing to offer you one and a quarter million dollars for sixteen percent of your shares in the Dansted Corporation. In addition, I'm sure we could come to an agreement about a specific job for you here. The company's big enough now to need a personnel manager."

She smiled. "Personnel managers went out with manual typewriters, Dan. They're called 'directors of human resources' nowadays. And they get much bigger offices than they used to."

"Whatever. Are you interested in selling those shares, Corinne?"

She had never expected him to make such a generous offer, and she hesitated, uncertain how to react. "That would mean I'd lose control of the company," she said, stalling.

"That's true. But another way of looking at my offer is to say that you would make a great deal of money while still retaining control of thirty-five percent of the shares. With that big a stake in the company, you know your opinions would be listened to."

"But not necessarily acted upon."

"But not necessarily acted upon," he agreed. "Our positions would be reversed. If we disagreed over something important, my opinion would automatically win out. On the other hand, you would be more than a million dollars richer."

He came back to stand in front of her again. His appearance seemed outwardly casual, but she could feel the tension radiating from him. Dan Matthews, she realized, wanted control of the Dansted Corporation very badly indeed.

"I'm sorry," she said. "The thought of all that money is very tempting, but control of the company means more to me than a million dollars. Charlie left me quite well provided for."

Dan's mouth tightened into a grim line. "I don't think you know what you're getting into, Corinne. Running a business isn't just an exciting extension of your college courses, you know."

"I don't imagine it is."

"Corinne, I'm not trying to put you down. I'm trying to explain some harsh facts to you. While you were in college, you probably studied various case histories of business organizations that were in the process of change, and you probably enjoyed solving the problems those cases presented. But the problems you'll be meeting when you start work with the Dansted Corporation aren't part of a classroom study. They're real problems. If you give the wrong answer, you won't get a bad grade on the course, you'll damage this company. And if you give enough wrong answers, you won't fail a course, you'll destroy Dansted."

"Dan, you're assuming we'll disagree on every—"

"I'm not assuming anything," he broke in. "I'm just pointing out the difference between playing Monopoly and conducting business in the real world. When you make a wrong decision on the Monopoly board, you lose some pieces of colored paper. In the real world, wrong decisions end up hurting people. This company directly employs a hundred and fifty people. It indirectly employs hundreds more. If you guess wrong too many times, Corinne, those people will eventually be unemployed."

She turned to stare out the window, wanting to escape the intensity of his expression. She wished Dan Matthews would return to the tidy pigeonhole where she'd kept him filed for most of the last seven years. She wanted him neatly labeled as a heartless workaholic with a great body and a well-trained mind. She didn't want his personality to take on any subtle and distracting layers of complexity.

A dirty white pigeon in the parking lot was pecking away at an invisible feast of crumbs, and she stared at it fixedly. The silence in the room stretched out as she watched the pigeon peck up the last crumb and fly away.

Corinne turned around. Dan was studying the drawing on the drafting board, but he looked up at the sound of her movement. She kept her gaze fixed on the middle of his shirt, not wanting to look into his eyes now that she had made her decision.

She was aware of a strange tremble of anticipation spreading out from her stomach, making her hands and knees shake. She hadn't expected this moment to arrive quite so soon, and she was nowhere near as calm as she would have liked.

"Dan," she said slowly, hoping he wouldn't hear the tiny quiver in her voice. The less emotion that entered into their negotiations, the easier it would be for both of them. "Would you care to have dinner with me this evening? I have a proposition you might find interesting."

Chapter Three

CORINNE PLUGGED IN the hair dryer and stared glumly at her reflection in the mirror. The closer it got to seven o'clock, the more anxious she felt about the next couple of hours. She stretched her mouth into a smile that was supposed to be simultaneously dignified and cheerful. When her jaw started to ache, she admitted defeat and decided to practice some small talk instead.

"Hello, Dan, so glad you could make it. This restaurant specializes in seafood. I've had the shrimp, and they were quite good. By the way, Charlie told me your first marriage was such a disaster that you no longer believe in marrying for love. How do you feel about marrying for convenience?"

She frowned. That was definitely not the casual conversation opener she was looking for. Throwing a man's previous marital failure in his face was hardly the way to win him over.

She gazed into the mirror again, wondering how actors always managed to look so warm and sincere. Her smile looked like a second-rate advertisement for dental floss. She lifted her long hair and directed hot air from the dryer toward the nape of her neck.

"Well, Dan, I'm sure you'd like me to get straight to the point! My parents' marriage was so totally lousy that

I'm terrified of committing myself to a long-term relationship with a man. However, I desperately want a baby. How would you feel about providing stud service?"

The mirrored image greeted her suggestion stonily. Corinne bit her lip, smothering a gasp of faintly hysterical laughter. Oh God! She really wanted this evening to turn out right!

She switched off the dryer and padded out of the bathroom, hesitating in front of the closet for several minutes before selecting a thin cotton dress with a plunging neckline and long sleeves. What suppressed Freudian impulses did that particular combination reveal? she wondered, then carefully thrust all thoughts of her appearance out of her mind. She had decided weeks ago that this project with Dan would never work if she allowed herself to relate to him in any of the traditional male/female ways. It would be easier for both of them if the whole thing was treated strictly as a business transaction.

When she entered the motel lobby, Dan was already downstairs waiting. He didn't see her immediately and, as she walked toward him, she noticed again the obvious strength behind his handsome features. A rush of unexpected emotion made her throat tighten and her mouth turn dry. Nerves, she told herself, and schooled her expression into the impersonal politeness that seemed to be her only defense against Dan Matthews.

He welcomed her with an equally polite smile and a few casual words of greeting, but she saw his hand resting on the bar rail and noticed that his knuckles were white with tension. From her point of view, that was a distinctly promising sign. Dan was obviously hoping she'd offer some sort of deal on her company shares, which meant he was likely to be receptive to her plan.

They exchanged social pleasantries as he escorted her into the motel dining room. He commented on the fact that the menu was extensive and reasonably priced. She remarked on the comfort of her room. They both ordered fish and saffron rice, and Dan selected a bottle of California chablis. Corinne allowed the waiter to fill her glass, but she was careful to sip the wine slowly. Having watched her mother drink herself to death, she had a self-imposed limit of one glass a night.

Once the waiter departed, Dan's flow of social chitchat stopped and he leaned back in his chair, waiting for her to make the next move. All at once she realized she wanted to know more about him before presenting her proposal. Aside from the fact that he was divorced and that Charlie had thought he was wonderful, she knew very little about his background. She was surprised at how much she wanted to fill in some of the blanks. "Charlie told me you went to college in Colorado," she said finally. "How did you enjoy living out West?"

"Very much. I wasn't crazy about Denver, but the Rocky Mountains must be one of the world's most spectacular sights. I used to spend my winter weekends skiing and the summer weekends rock-climbing or white-water rafting. It was a great life. How about you? Is your family from Colorado?"

"Yes, my mother and father were both born in Grand Junction." She was so accustomed to avoiding talk about her parents that she switched the conversation back to Dan almost without thinking. "Did you ever consider settling in Colorado?" she asked.

"I thought about it a lot. But I married two weeks after I finished school, and Mary Beth wanted to be near her family and friends on the East Coast. So I came back to Rhode Island with her."

"The Dansted Corporation's been such a success that I guess you don't regret the decision."

"No," he said slowly. "Although I've often regretted the way it was made."

"You mean you regret having given in to Mary Beth's wishes?"

"No, not exactly. But I bitterly regret the fact that we were both too young and infatuated to realize what sort of a relationship we were setting up with each other. The way we decided to leave Colorado was typical of virtually every decision we made in our marriage. Mary Beth cajoled and I resisted. She nagged and then—finally—I gave in. But I never had the maturity or the common sense to give in with good grace."

Corinne hesitated. She hadn't meant to get onto such intimate ground quite so soon. "Charlie told me once that your marriage was very unhappy."

Dan gave a short laugh. "That's one of Charlie's rare cases of understatement. My marriage to Mary Beth wasn't merely unhappy—it was a full-fledged disaster."

Corinne took another small sip of her wine. "Because of her constant nagging?" she asked neutrally.

His gaze was shrewd, almost amused. "I'm mature enough to realize that it takes two to ruin a marriage," he said. "While I was going through our divorce, I blamed Mary Beth for every bad thing that had ever happened to me. If I could have found some way to blame her for the trouble I had cutting my baby teeth, I'd have done it. But I realized quite some time ago that she's a decent enough woman. Her only real problem was that she married the wrong man."

The young waiter slipped two platters of steaming, golden-coated fish before them with instructions to enjoy their meal. Dan offered Corinne the tartar sauce and, when she refused, heaped a generous helping onto his own plate.

Corinne avoided meeting Dan's eyes. "Sometimes I think there's a lot to be said for the old system of arranged marriages," she suggested, her heart beginning to pound as she nudged the conversation in the direction of her proposal. "I often think Victorian parents couldn't have done a worse job of picking mates for their children than we do for ourselves."

"As far as Mary Beth and I are concerned, you're probably right. I guess we were a classic example of the pitfalls of the modern mating system. We met at a student dance and fell instantly in love—whatever that means. Six months later we decided to get married. Unfortunately, we reached our decision without ever getting out of bed long enough to discover we had nothing going for us except fireworks in the bedroom."

Corinne felt an inexplicable surge of jealousy, although she had no idea why she should be troubled by the thought of Dan and Mary Beth enjoying a passionate sexual relationship. She forced herself to speak lightly. "I thought psychologists claim that if a couple is compatible in bed they can learn to be compatible anywhere."

"Even psychologists can't be that crazy," he said with a faint grin. "Mary Beth and I were unsuited in almost every way. She wanted a husband who'd keep her in luxury, but who'd be home by six o'clock every night. I wanted to prove I was the hottest businessman to come down the pike since Lee Iacocca. We soon found there was no way to reconcile our different needs and, to be honest, I don't think either of us was grown up enough to try very hard. I saw that she was bored, but the only solution I could come up with was to suggest she get a job of her own. I never stopped to consider that following her own career wasn't what Mary Beth wanted out of life."

Corinne had somehow assumed that Dan was chiefly responsible for the breakup of his marriage. She was now beginning to think it was a miracle he'd managed to stay married for five long years.

"Did Mary Beth complain about the demands of your job?" she asked with newly felt sympathy.

"I guess so," he said, "but with good reason. When I wasn't on the road, trying to set up a sales network, I was barricaded in the factory fixing glitches on the production line. We hardly ever saw each other." He smiled ruefully. "And it didn't help that I was in the plumbing business. Mary Beth might have tolerated taking second place behind something glamorous like antique furniture, but competing with a bunch of sump pumps was more than she could bear. I think she had her first affair more to convince herself that she was a desirable woman than to hurt me."

"Her first affair?"

He shrugged. "After she'd enjoyed one, I guess taking lovers became a habit. I think she was almost relieved the night I came home unexpectedly early and found her in bed with the country-club tennis pro."

Hearing the lingering echo of pain in Dan's voice, Corinne deliberately made her response light. "She might at least have chosen somebody more original. Didn't she know that the tennis pro is a positive cliché?"

Dan's mouth twisted with a hint of self-mockery. "I think she'd already worked her way through everybody more exciting. And as she pointed out at the time, if I'd been home more often, it wouldn't have taken me so long to find out what was going on."

Corinne experienced a crazy urge to comfort him.

"You shouldn't blame yourself too much, Dan. If you'd been home more, you and Mary Beth would probably have argued about something else. When two people aren't compatible, they can always find something to fight about."

"You sound as if you're talking from experience."

"Sort of. My parents were as unsuited as you and Mary Beth," she admitted honestly. "Only they weren't smart enough to get a divorce. I think my earliest childhood memory is of pulling the bedcovers over my head so I wouldn't have to hear my father shouting and my mother crying."

"But you were happy in your marriage to my uncle," Dan said, a faint question in his voice.

She felt her mouth soften into an involuntary smile. "Charlie was different," she said. "Our marriage was special." She looked up, meeting Dan's eyes. "Charlie and I did everything the wrong way around," she said. "We married for strictly practical reasons and ended up loving each other more than we'd ever imagined possible. Maybe that's why I think some of those Victorian parents had the right idea. Personally, I've come to the conclusion that falling in love is a very risky basis for getting married. I'd say mutual self-interest is by far the safest foundation for any relationship."

"Is that what your marriage to Charlie was based upon? Mutual self-interest?"

"In a way." She had a feeling that Dan was about to start asking some questions she wasn't ready or willing to answer, so she said quickly, "I hope you're planning to order dessert. They make the best chocolate-fudge sundaes here I've ever tasted."

The look he directed toward her was rapier sharp, but he accepted her change of subject without comment, talking entertainingly about his recent trip to China while they waited for dessert to arrive. When they had both made some inroads into their mounds of whipped cream and thick, dripping chocolate, he put down his spoon and regarded her levelly.

"Corinne, I've enjoyed this dinner, but when we set it up you said you had a proposition to put to me. I assume it's something to do with the Dansted Corporation. Are you ready to tell me what you have in mind?"

Corinne hid her hands in her lap so he couldn't see they were shaking. "Yes, I'm ready," she said, relieved to note that her voice sounded more or less under control. "It concerns Charlie's will. I'm sure you remember the terms."

"I remember the terms with crystal clarity."

She reached for her water glass and took a large swallow. "Well then, you'll no doubt recall that one of the conditions was that if I married again, you would have the automatic right to buy up all my shares in the Dansted Corporation for a million dollars."

"I remember."

"Charlie made that provision because he didn't want control of the company to end up in some outsider's hands."

"I appreciate his thoughtfulness," Dan said dryly.

His brusque answers weren't helping at all. She unwound her fingers from the tight knot she'd tied them in. "Your bankers were prepared to authorize a loan of three million dollars to buy me out, so I'm sure you'll agree that a price of only one million is a real bargain."

His silvery-gray eyes narrowed in sudden, intent speculation. "It certainly is," he said. "But unless you're planning to marry again, it's a bargain that does me no good."

He had finally given her the perfect opening, yet her throat obstinately closed up as if determined to keep her proposition unsaid. She reached for her glass of water again, but even after she drank half of it, her throat still felt as dry as sandpaper.

When she didn't say anything more, Dan picked up his spoon and stirred it thoughtfully in the remains of his melting sundae. "In view of the opinions about marriage you've just expressed, I'd be astonished if you were thinking of marrying again in the near future."

Corinne's stomach still felt as if it were trying to take a high dive into the soles of her feet, but she stared hard at the buttons on Dan's sport coat and forced herself to speak. "It's possible that in certain circumstances I might be prepared to get married again," she said. "In fact, I might be prepared to get married quite soon."

"Precisely what circumstances would tempt you back to the altar, Corinne?"

Some almost indiscernible tremor in the timbre of his voice made her look up. His face was absolutely devoid of expression, but that very lack of emotion made her see just how tense he was. He wasn't deliberately trying to intimidate her, she reallized. He was being cool and abrupt because he was afraid to reveal how important the conversation was to him. Oddly enough, the simple knowledge that he was as uptight as she was gave Corinne the courage to carry on.

She cleared her throat. "I would be willing to marry you as soon as we could arrange for a license," she said. Her voice, thank heaven, hadn't even wavered. "Control of the Dansted Corporation would then pass directly into your hands."

Silence stretched out endlessly between them. Glancing up, she had to admire his extraordinary self-control.

No wonder he was so brilliantly successful in trade negotiations, she thought irrelevantly. She managed to detect no more than a brief flare of total astonishment before his eyes narrowed and his feelings were once again concealed behind an expressionless mask.

"I'm extremely flattered by your proposal," he said at last. "But I'm also a little curious. My track record as a husband isn't exactly dazzling, so would you mind explaining why you find me such an attractive prospect that you're willing to toss away two million dollars and control of the Dansted Corporation in order to get me?"

She drew in a deep breath. "There's a condition to the marriage," she said.

"Ah, of course! A condition. And that is . . . ?"

With a supreme effort of will, she kept her voice cool and her gaze steady. "It's a very simple one," she said. "All you have to do is sign a prenuptial document agreeing to stay married long enough for me to get pregnant and give birth to your child."

Chapter Four

DAN FELT HIS hand jerk against his cup, spilling coffee into the saucer, and he knew that his jaw had quite literally dropped. Corinne had finally succeeded in shattering the rigid control he had so far kept over his emotions. Several seconds passed before he managed to close his mouth and straighten in his chair.

When his capacity for thought returned, he immediately wondered about her real purpose in making such a crazy proposal. The image of Corinne Steddon as desperate for motherhood simply didn't fit with his impression of her character. From the time of their first meeting, everything about her behavior suggested she craved the sensation of power that came from running a successful international company. But if commercial power was what she wanted, surely she wouldn't deliberately seek the disruption and inconvenience of pregnancy and maternity. Whichever way he looked at it, her proposition made no sense at all.

"Let me make sure I've understood you correctly," he said finally. "You agree to sell me your shares in the Dansted Corporation for one million dollars, and all I have to do in exchange is get you pregnant."

"Not quite all," Corinne said. "You have to marry me first, and we have to stay married until the baby is born.

That way you have the security of knowing that we've taken care of the legal clauses in Charlie's will, and my baby has the advantage of being born into a conventional family setting."

Dan remained silent for a few moments as he studied her. If his taste had happened to run to tall blondes with classic features, he would have found Corinne Steddon a remarkably good-looking woman. As it happened, his personal preference was more for cute, cuddly brunettes, but even he wasn't entirely immune to Corinne's sensual impact. She had the sort of curvaceous feminine body that was guaranteed to send any red-blooded male racing right off into fantasyland. If he was honest with himself, he would have to admit he had spent a fair part of their dinner trying not to notice the appealing huskiness of her voice and the enticing thrust of her breasts against the low neckline of her dress. And despite his preference for brown eyes, the deep clear blue of hers was surprisingly appealing. Oddly enough, the expression in her eyes wasn't sexy, he decided, or at least not consciously so. In fact, if he hadn't known better, he would have said her gaze displayed a rather quaint sort of innocence.

Dan redirected his thoughts with a cynical mental shrug. Corinne's delightful physical attributes only made her proposal even more preposterous than it otherwise might have been. Why in the world was such an attractive woman making him such an extraordinary offer? She could undoubtedly have walked into any singles bar in Denver and found a minimum of two dozen men only too delighted to impregnate her. Why on earth had she selected him?

"Two million dollars in exchange for a marriage license," he said neutrally. "That's quite a stud fee, Corinne. But honesty compels me to point out that there are much cheaper ways of getting yourself pregnant than by buying my services."

"I appreciate the advice," she replied politely. "However, I've given the matter a great deal of thought, and my offer still stands."

Dan suppressed an irritated sigh, wondering why women never seemed capable of saying straightforwardly what was on their minds. His mother and his ex-wife were both masterly in their ability to conceal their real demands behind layers of confusing camouflage, and he was sure Corinne had some devious plan perking somewhere in the recesses of her soul. One thing he knew for sure: her proposal couldn't be taken at face value. This was a woman who had not only married a man forty years her senior but, by her own admission, had married him for his money. Clearly, it would be prudent for him to find out precisely what subterfuges her proposal really concealed; otherwise he might wake up one sunny morning and discover that Corinne Steddon was the new owner of a hundred percent of the Dansted Corporation shares.

"Marriage and parenthood were just about the last things I had planned for the next few months," he said, forcing a casual smile. He wondered how she would react if he was actually crazy enough to agree to her proposition. It would almost be worth pretending to accept her terms, just to find out what she was really up to. "On the other hand, your proposal certainly has some intriguing aspects."

She leaned forward across the table, affording him a spectacular view of her breasts. Her face lit up with such eagerness that some men might have been naïve enough to think she really didn't know just how much of her cleavage was revealed. Dan, however, tossed her a sardonic mental compliment and settled down to enjoy the view. Years of tough international negotiations had taught him to enjoy life's little pleasures while in no way allowing them to distract him.

"The point is, it wouldn't be a real marriage or real parenthood for you," Corinne said earnestly. "The sort of marriage I'm talking about would make almost no difference to your lifestyle. Think of it this way, Dan. If you agree to my proposal, you'll be committed to spending a few nights with me—maybe a dozen or so over a period of three months. But in exchange for that tiny investment of your time, you'll gain complete control of the Dansted Corporation, and at bargain basement prices."

"It's certainly a tempting thought," he said neutrally. "Except that I also acquire a wife and child along with the control of my company."

"But only a temporary wife. We'll draw up detailed prenuptial agreements with our lawyers, making it clear that we're free to divorce each other as soon as the baby is born."

Was that her plan? he wondered. Did she intend to hire a smart lawyer and take him to the cleaners when it came time for their divorce?

"Prenuptial agreements don't always stand up in court," he pointed out. "With a good lawyer and the right divorce judge, you could probably win the return of all your shares and keep the million dollars I paid you as an extra little bonus for the—quote—'heartache' of your failed marriage."

She shrugged impatiently. "Dan, I'm not trying to cheat you. Once those company shares are yours, I have no intention of trying to get them back. You can ask Frank to draw up the agreement so it's absolutely watertight from your point of view. He's an honest, reputable lawyer, and you've worked with him for years. I swear I won't dispute any clause he comes up with for your financial protection."

Dan stirred uncomfortably in his seat. God help him, but he was beginning to think this crazy woman was actually on the level. He spoke curtly. "Even if we managed to dissolve the marriage without any surprises, I think you're forgetting something rather important, Corinne. I would still be the father of your child."

"I hadn't forgotten that," she said quietly. "As far as the baby is concerned, you can make whatever sort of commitment to paternity you want. You don't have to feel obligated to care for my baby just because you agreed to be its biological father. You needn't be anything more than a name on the birth certificate."

"Do you think that's fair to the child?"

"No, not entirely, but I've given this matter a lot of thought, Dan. I've read books by single parents of both sexes, and I'm confident that I can provide my child with sufficient love to compensate for the fact that he or she will be growing up in a one-parent family. On the other hand, if you would like to have occasional visitation rights, I wouldn't object. I've always heard that most men have a tough time relating to very young babies, but if you wanted to have the child spend summer vacations with you in a few years, I'd be perfectly willing to work out some sort of an arrangement."

"In writing, with the lawyers?"

If he hadn't known better, he would have sworn he saw hurt in her eyes before she looked away. "If you think that's necessary."

Dan poured himself another glass of wine and leaned back in his chair. Could her proposition possibly be nothing more than what it seemed on the surface—an offer to sell him her shares in exchange for his agreement to make her pregnant? For a brief, unwilling moment, he found himself considering what it would be like to make love to Corinne. He imagined her long legs spread out beneath him, her breasts lying heavy in his palms, and her long hair tossed haphazardly across the pillow. He felt his mouth moving urgently over her parted lips and heard her moan of excitement when he finally entered her body. He visualized her breasts swelling with the onset of pregnancy, and her flat stomach growing hard and round with his child. To his astonishment, he found the image of a pregnant Corinne extremely arousing. He hurriedly pulled his chair closer to the table in an effort to conceal just how arousing.

"Corinne," he said, "I'm going to level with you. When Frank and I first heard the terms of Charlie's will, we both thought the best thing that could happen to the Dansted Corporation was for you to get married again as soon as possible." He smiled wryly. "I made a list of all my bachelor friends and estimated how long it would take to introduce every one of them to you. But I never considered putting myself on the list. Believe me, Corinne, I'd make a lousy husband and a worse father."

"I don't care what sort of husband you'd make, and Charlie told me that your family has outstanding genes. He said you have two older sisters, each with a clutch of brilliant, bright-eyed offspring."

"Dammit all, Corinne! There's more to being a father than impregnating an egg with a supply of sound genes! It may have escaped your notice, but most people find parenthood works out better if you fall in love and get married before you start planning to have a baby."

She stared into the middle distance, refusing to meet his eyes. "You know my opinion of love as a basis for marriage," she said.

"Okay, so maybe marriage isn't for you. I'm not all

that wild about it myself. But you could wait until you fall in love with a guy and then let him become the father. At least that way your child would be conceived in love, even if neither of you felt able to make a long-term commitment to the relationship."

"I considered that possibility," Corinne said. "But I'm twenty-six, Dan, and I want to have a baby before I'm too old to enjoy the experience. Who knows how long I'd have to wait before I found a suitable lover? Once you introduce emotions into the scene, the whole picture starts to get cluttered up. For example, what happens if I fall in love but the man in question doesn't want to become a father?"

"Women have been getting pregnant for years without telling the men what they're doing."

He was surprised to see how much his careless words upset her. "Well, I would *never* do that," she said vehemently. "I've seen what happens when a woman traps a man with a child he doesn't want, and it's torment for all three of them. I think men have as much right as women to share in the decision to become a parent."

"All right, I agree with you, but don't you think you might be creating difficulties where none exist? I'd guess that most men are as anxious to have a child as most women. Why should you expect to fall in love with one of the few men in the world who doesn't want to become a father?"

As she brushed a strand of golden hair away from her cheeks, Dan found himself following the movement of her fingers. Her skin was as softly luminous as the inside of a shell. How would it feel to touch it? he wondered.

"I think what I'm really scared of is the possibility that I might never fall in love," she continued. "The fact is, I'm like you, Dan. I'm not sure I even know what the words mean. Charlie and I cared about each other very deeply, but we never felt any of the sensations songwriters and movie-makers are always going on about. Then take your own case, Dan. You thought you were in love with Mary Beth, yet a few months after you were married you both bitterly regretted what you'd done. My mother thought she was in love with my father, but she had to drink herself into oblivion every night simply to tolerate the pain of living with him. I've decided there must be a more practical way of choosing a father for my baby than waiting to fall in love."

"Even if I agree with some of what you're saying, I still can't understand why you want me to be the father. To be honest, Corinne, I'd have thought I was just about the last man to find himself on your list of prospective fathers."

"You're not looking at this from my point of view," she said. "I can't recruit a father for my baby by walking into the street and offering the job to the first decent-looking man who walks by."

Dan's voice became very dry. "Believe me, Corinne, you won't have to take to the streets. You'll have a waiting list of qualified applicants a mile long as soon as you pass the word that you're willing to pay two million dollars for the services of the successful applicant."

A hint of rueful laughter darkened her eyes. "And exactly where do you suggest I go to pass the word? A singles bar? My neighborhood health club? Maybe my local church? Our minister is a great guy, but I somehow don't think he'd be too supportive if I tried placing an ad in the church newsletter stating my desire for immediate motherhood and requesting healthy volunteers for the role of impregnator to please step forward."

"You could take a family doctor or lawyer into your confidence and ask him to screen candidates."

"I suppose I could do that." She regarded him with unexpected shyness, and for some reason he felt his heart give a strange, uncomfortable lurch. "But your uncle spoke about you with so much pride that you seemed the ideal candidate. Charlie was forever boasting about your brilliant high-school and college record, you know. Whenever he met somebody new, he always found a way to tell them how you went to college on an athletic scholarship and won the Western Region Tennis Championship the same semester you made straight A's."

To his amazement, Dan felt himself redden. It had to be years since he'd last blushed. "Did Charlie also remember to tell everybody that I made straight C's as a freshman and almost lost my scholarship?"

She laughed. "No, he glossed over that bit. But I'm glad to hear you aren't totally perfect." She drew her forefinger around the rim of her empty coffee cup. "I'll be honest with you, Dan. From everything Charlie told me, genetically speaking you seem like the ideal father for my child, and his will has given me the leverage I needed to make the deal attractive to you."

Dan couldn't conceal a spurt of incredulity. "Are you telling me Charlie *knew* about this scheme of yours?"

She hesitated before answering him. "No," she said finally. "Charlie had his own reasons for writing the will as he did, but he had no inkling of how I planned to use it."

Once again Dan fell silent, staring into the melting blobs of his ice cream as if he hoped they would give him inspiration. He didn't like to admit, even to himself, how tempting Corinne's offer sounded. After all, he reasoned, he had always hoped to become a father sometime in the dim and distant future. Would it be so bad to give Corinne the child she wanted in exchange for full control of his own company? Several crucial business decisions would have to be made in the near future, and he couldn't afford to have Corinne voting against him. When you got right down to basics, maybe he had an *obligation* to impregnate the wretched woman and keep his company safe.

Fortunately, his sense of humor reasserted itself. He would be in big trouble if he ever managed to convince himself it was his duty to father a child for some woman he scarcely knew and didn't really like.

"Corinne," he said quickly, "I'm sorry, but I can't go along with your plan. There's no way I can agree to become the father of your child."

"I see," she said. "Would you mind telling me why?"

"Lots of reasons," he replied quietly. "You and I are adults, Corinne, and we're entitled to make any decisions we please concerning our personal lives. But what about the child you're suggesting we create? How do you think he would feel when he discovered he was born as the result of a deal between his parents for the shares in a plumbing-supplies company?"

"That's not how I would explain it to him," Corinne objected. "I would tell him he was born because both of us wanted him very much. And that would be the truth."

"No, it would only be a shaded version of the truth," Dan said. "I'm sorry, Corinne, but I've always considered half-truths to be even more dangerous than outright lies. I'll admit I'm tempted by your offer, but if I accepted, I'm certain we'd both regret it in the long run. Later on, when you meet somebody you love, you'll be glad you didn't use me to help create your baby." He smiled with deliberate self-mockery, wanting to ease the almost palpable tension between them. "Good Lord, I never knew I was so noble! I can't believe I'm actually turning down such an easy method of winning back those shares!"

"I must say I wish your conscience had turned out to be a little less sensitive," Corinne said coolly. "But thank you for explaining your position so honestly." She sounded very much in control of herself and her emotions. If she hadn't been so careful to avoid meeting his eyes, Dan would have thought she was completely indifferent to his refusal.

She gathered up her purse and summoned the waiter with a crisp nod of her head. The restaurant was almost empty, and the waiter arrived promptly. Dan pulled out his billfold and searched for a credit card to pay for their meal.

"No, please. It was my invitation, and I'd like to pay." She reached across the table, stopping his search. Though her fingers were cool, he felt an inexplicably warm tingle where they rested fleetingly against the back of his hand. Unaccountably, he found himself fighting an impulse to grasp her hand and hold it until her slender fingers lost their coolness and became warm and seeking and eager . . .

Dan pushed his wallet back into his pocket, feeling a touch of impatience with himself. "Well, many thanks for an enjoyable meal," he said. "I've never eaten here before, even though it's so close to the factory."

As the waiter left their table, it was on the tip of Dan's tongue to ask Corinne if she'd be willing to reconsider selling her shares in the Dansted Corporation. He thought of pointing out that with three million dollars in hard cash she could buy any number of extremely attractive solutions to the problem of finding a father for her baby. Somehow, though, he couldn't find any words that didn't sound unbearably crass. Something about her careful politeness, or perhaps the unconscious rigidity of her shoulders, touched some deeply buried protective chord. He found himself fighting an absurd impulse to take her into his arms and comfort her. Comfort her for what? he wondered. For his failure to agree to her totally crazy plan?

"Corinne," he said softly, "what happens now?"

"Speaking personally, I'm going back to my room to catch up on too many nights of too little sleep. These past few days have been ridiculously hectic." She nodded to the waiter as they walked out of the restaurant and headed toward the lobby. Her manner was so brisk that Dan began to wonder if he had imagined that earlier hint of vulnerability.

"Corinne, that's not what I meant."

She paused by the elevators and swung around to face him. "I'll be in the office at eight o'clock tomorrow morning, Dan, and I look forward to seeing you there. We have a great many business matters to discuss. I've already noticed several areas of company policy that could use my urgent attention."

Nobody had ever accused Dan of being slow on the uptake, and in a hard voice he said, "Is this your way of telling me that unless I agree to father your child, you're going to make it impossible for me to run the Dansted Corporation? Is that what you're threatening, Corinne?"

Her blue eyes opened wide as she fixed him with an infuriatingly innocent gaze. "How could you even think such a thing, Dan? Why, that would be blackmail."

The elevator arrived, and she stepped inside, giving him one final dazzling smile.

"Good night, Dan. Sleep well. I'll see you tomorrow morning."

Chapter Five

CORINNE OPENED THE door to the office Dan had assigned her the previous afternoon. Hot, humid air wafted out of the dark interior. She fumbled for the light switch, and overhead fluorescent strips gradually illuminated the drab walls. At least the room was large, she thought wryly.

The factory's centralized cooling system worked indifferently in this section of the building, and her cream linen jacket was already sticking to her back. After living in Colorado for twenty-six years, her body was having a hard time adjusting to the East Coast's pervasive humidity. Corinne crossed to the tiny office window and switched on the individual air-conditioning unit. It sputtered to life with a throaty, reluctant wheeze, and after a few seconds the noisy fan began blowing out a welcome stream of cool air.

She took off her jacket with a sigh of relief, hanging it on the metal hook which was all the room provided by way of a coat rack. She sat down at her desk, a steel monstrosity in a bilious shade of khaki that would have looked more at home in the reject section of an army surplus store. She leaned forward to switch on her reading lamp, taking great care to avoid the sharp desk corner which had snagged two pairs of hose yesterday and gouged out a sizable sliver of her shin for good measure.

Yesterday afternoon, when Debbie had first shown her into this office, Corinne had assumed Dan was deliberately making life difficult by assigning her the most uncomfortable workspace he could find. Having spent some time touring the other offices, however, she'd immediately acquitted him of any such evil intention. Dan's interests obviously centered exclusively on his factory, which was bright, streamlined, well ventilated, and aggressively efficient. By contrast, the environment for his clerks and managers was uniformly dreary. All the offices were at least as shabby as this one, and several were worse.

Her meditations were interrupted by a quick knock on her door. She barely had time to respond before Dan strode into the room.

"I've brought you the files on the company health plan," he said tersely. "Where would you like me to put them?"

She cleared a space on the corner of her desk for a wire in-tray. "Here would be fine, thanks."

She busied herself shuffling papers so that she wouldn't have to look at him. Somehow, though, she had already registered every detail of his appearance. He was wearing a navy blue suit, obviously custom-tailored, a white broadcloth shirt, and a sober blue and gray striped tie. She wondered why such conservative clothes should immediately cause her to wonder what it would feel like to touch the muscled body concealed beneath the impeccable tailoring.

There was only one chair in her office, and she was sitting on it, but Dan didn't seem to mind. She suspected he rarely stopped moving long enough to feel the need for a chair. She looked up when he stopped his restless pacing and gestured to the files on her desk.

"If you have any questions about our health plan, ask Alma Grady, my secretary. She knows most of the details—probably more than I do. I'm afraid I won't be available for the next few days. I've been unexpectedly summoned to Washington."

"No problems, I hope?"

"Not really, except that the timing's bad for me. I'm too busy to spend a week in Washington playing tour guide."

"Who are you going to guide?"

"Our government is sponsoring a trade delegation from Shanghai on a tour of the country. Since I've already met several of the Chinese officials who are over here, somebody at the Commerce Department came up with the bright idea of asking me to act as the government's unofficial host." His mouth moved in a sardonic grimace. "I think the Under Secretary expects me to squeeze in a few lectures on the blessings of capitalism, in between our trips to Capitol Hill and the Washington Monument."

"Well, that should be easy enough, Dan. Treat your visitors to lunch at a fast-food restaurant and tell them that if all the peasants work hard, within five years they can have food just like that all over China."

He laughed. "I think the Under Secretary might decide I was being subversive." His expression sobered. "Corinne, as far as the Dansted Corporation is concerned, several major decisions are pending—"

"Don't worry," she put in quickly. "I still have a lot to learn about the company, and I don't plan to question your judgment on any of the issues that are currently under consideration."

"Do I have your word on that?"

"Yes, you have my word."

He walked toward the door, then swung around to

face her. "Corinne, about last night..."

"Dan, please don't give it another moment's thought," she said with a convincing pretense of casualness. He must never guess how much effort it cost her to look him straight in the eye and smile serenely. "Having slept on it, I've decided that my proposal was a mistake. Being a career woman is much more to my taste than becoming a single mother. I would really like you to forget our discussion."

"I'm glad you feel that way. I'm sure you'll be glad you decided not to go ahead with your plan."

His eyes raked her once, swiftly, and she dropped her gaze. She had known it would be difficult meeting Dan this morning, but she had underestimated the problem by a wide margin. For one thing, she hadn't expected her throat to turn dry and her palms damp simply at the sight of him. She didn't have much practical experience of sexual desire, but she had enough theoretical knowledge to recognize what was causing the weird, almost painful knotting in her stomach.

"I guess I'll see you next week," she said with a brightness that sounded forced even to her own ears.

"I'll look forward to it," he said, and the hard lines of his mouth softened momentarily into a smile. "I promise you'll be the first person to hear how the folks from Shanghai liked french fries and chocolate milk shakes."

As soon as his footsteps faded into silence, she got up and pushed the door shut, leaning against it as she wiped her palms on a tissue. Several seconds passed before her knees stopped shaking. She wouldn't have had a problem, she thought, if only he hadn't smiled.

What was so special about Dan Matthews, anyway? True, he was spectacularly good looking, but lots of other men were just as handsome. True, he was tall and muscular, but lots of other men had better bodies. Well, right off the top of her head she couldn't think of anyone who had a better body. True, Dan's hair was thick and glossy, but it was a perfectly ordinary shade of brown. And just because his gray eyes sometimes gleamed with an intriguing, captivating hint of silver, that was no reason for her limbs to turn all soft and heavy every time he looked at her.

Her desire for a child must be investing Dan Matthews with a totally false appeal, Corinne decided. Her strange reaction to him was undoubtedly just the result of overactive hormones, and with the exercise of a little self-discipline she would soon have her wayward emotions under complete control. She tossed the crumpled tissue into the gray metal wastebasket and walked purposefully across the room. It was time to catch up on her background reading.

She sat down at her desk and opened the file containing a breakdown of projected sales figures for the month of June. They certainly looked promising. If the second half of the year was as profitable as the first, the Dansted Corporation would declare a record profit.

Corinne leaned back in her chair. She hadn't lied to Dan when she said she had no intention of interfering with any important business decisions while he was out of town. But she had lied when she said she'd given up on her plan for motherhood. In fact, she was becoming more and more convinced that Dan would make an ideal father for her baby. For some reason, though, she wasn't anxious to define precisely what characteristics made him so well qualified for the role.

She glanced down at the open file before her and frowned. Ever since Charlie had encouraged her to go back to school and get her degree, she had prided herself on her powers of concentration, but today that concentration seemed sorely lacking. She was supposed to be learning everything she could about the Dansted Corporation, not daydreaming about her baby-to-be. So far, everything she had seen suggested that Dan ran his company with a dedication and an insight that bordered on commercial genius. It was going to be difficult to come up with ways to get under his skin without damaging the profitability or the reputation of the company.

She leaned across the desk to retrieve the group insurance files Dan had left in her in-tray, but she had forgotten the hidden perils of the ancient desk. There was an ominous ripping sound as the protruding metal brace on the file drawer skewered her stocking, simultaneously inflicting yet another bruise onto her already battered leg. She jumped to her feet, swearing colorfully under her breath.

"May I come in?" Frank Goldberg, the company lawyer, appeared in her doorway. "Although something tells me this isn't the best time for a visit."

"Of course you can come in," she said, smiling a welcome. "In fact, you're just the person I need to see. In my opinion, this darned desk should be registered as a lethal weapon." She pointed to her shredded stocking and to the thin trickle of blood seeping through the ruined mesh. "I've been mortally wounded. How do you rate my chances of success if I sue the company for damages?"

Frank's thin features immediately assumed an expression of lawyerlike caution. "It would be a great deal easier just to order a new desk," he replied, obviously unwilling to treat the subject of lawsuits lightly. "But my word, Corinne, that bruise looks nasty. Do you think you should see the nurse?"

Corinne only registered his first few words. "Of course!" she exclaimed, beaming at him delightedly. "Buy a new desk! Why in the world didn't *I* think of that? Frank, what a simply wonderful idea!"

"Really?" Frank's voice became even more cautious. "Naturally, I'm delighted to have been of service." He cleared his throat. "Mrs. Steddon . . . Corinne . . . Dan just left to catch his flight for Washington, and he asked me to take care of any questions you might have, or to help with any problems that might come up while he's away."

"That was very thoughtful of him," Corinne said absently. She was so pleased to have found a solution to her problem that she scarcely heard what Frank was saying. Redecorating Dansted Corporation headquarters wouldn't damage the company in any way. On the contrary, she'd be performing a definite service. However, from what little she knew of Dan Matthews, he would go quietly crazy within two days after falling over his first painter. And before long, he'd be prepared to pay almost any price to get rid of her.

Coming out of her reverie, she gave Frank a brilliant smile. "As it happens, Frank, I could use your help right away. I'm going to follow your advice and buy myself a new desk. Perhaps you could suggest a good place to find one."

"With pleasure. I'll ask Debbie to call a few stores and request some catalogs; then you can make your choice without ever having to leave the comfort of the building."

Corinne smiled wryly. "You know, Frank, unlike you old-timers, I don't find Dansted Corporation headquarters all that comfortable. It's obviously way past time for the company to redecorate, so I plan to hire painters and buy new furniture for everybody, not just for me." She felt herself warming to her theme. "Maybe we could

check out some good, sturdy carpeting while we're looking around. The linoleum in several of the offices is so
worn that it's dangerous."

He stared at her in horror. "Redecorate?" he exclaimed. "We've never decorated the offices here!"

"Frank," she said gently, "that is only too obvious."

He flushed angrily. "This is a plumbing-supplies company," he said stiffly. "We're not an advertising agency
or anything glamorous like that. Our clients don't expect
to find fancy wallpaper and plush carpets when they come
here. They expect to find the best plumbing hardware in
the country, and that's exactly what they get."

"Frank, the people in this company spend a great deal
of time reminding me that the Dansted Corporation sells
plumbing supplies. Please take my word for it, I understand what the company sells. But there's no reason why
these offices can't be made a great deal more pleasant
to work in, regardless of our product."

The lawyer's shoulders hunched obstinately. "Have
you discussed this with Dan?"

"No," she said, managing to keep her voice completely cool. "It was your suggestion about buying a new
desk that just gave me the idea to redecorate."

Frank didn't attempt to disguise his dismay. "Well, I
certainly never meant to suggest a major remodeling of
the offices! You completely misunderstood me, Corinne.
I'm sure Dan would never approve. He's always plowed
most of the profits straight back into the production line.
After all, the factory is the heart of our business, not the
clerical offices."

"I quite agree, and I'm sure that when the company
was just getting started there was no money to spare for
fancy office furniture. Although, however short of cash
you were, I think Dan could have had the office walls
painted some cheerier color than fungus green."

"The painting contractor told us this was a very durable shade," Frank said defensively.

"I'll just bet he did," Corinne muttered. "He'd probably been trying to palm it off on somebody for years. But that's not the point, Frank. The point is that the Dansted Corporation isn't short of ready cash at the moment, and there's no reason for anybody to work in these gloomy surroundings any longer. I could show you a dozen different studies that conclusively prove people work more efficiently in a pleasant environment."

Frank smiled placatingly. "Well, it's very hot out Corinne, and I wouldn't recommend traipsing around furniture warehouses today. We'll ask Debbie to call and request those brochures I talked about, and then, when Dan gets back from Washington, you can make your recommendations to him and see what he says. I'm sure if you put your case to him convincingly, he'll agree to authorize the purchase of a few new desks."

Corinne counted silently to ten, then walked over to the rusty wall hook and donned her jacket with careful, deliberate movements. She allowed the silence to stretch out until the room vibrated with its tension.

"Frank," she said finally, keeping her voice low and controlled, "as the majority shareholder in this company, I believe I have the authority to buy as many desks as I want. I plan to visit some office furniture companies this afternoon. Would you care to join me?"

Frank couldn't have looked less enthusiastic if she had asked him to join the devil in a dance at a church social. "Yes, of course, Corinne," he said miserably. "I'd be happy to recommend a couple of reputable suppliers."

When Corinne arrived at the office at seven o'clock on Monday morning, she found two carpenters already at work installing a skylight over the reception desk in the main entrance. She nodded cheerfully to them, lugging her suitcase around a ladder and several buckets of paint as she weaved her way down the corridor. Opening the door to her office, she gave a huge grin, hugging herself with almost childlike excitement.

She had spent most of the previous week dashing in and out of furniture stores while the painters and carpet-layers transformed her office. Even though she had watched every stage of their efforts, Corinne could still hardly believe the results. She dragged her suitcase into the middle of the room and stared around her with wide-eyed pleasure.

The old air-conditioner was gone, replaced by a smaller and infinitely quieter modern unit. The floor was covered with Berber wool carpet of soft beige, and the walls glowed in a delicate shade of ivory. A functional teak-wood desk and matching credenza were flanked by two small sofas, each covered in a beige and ivory fabric and dotted with peach-colored cushions. The once empty floor space in the center of the room was now filled by a small coffee table, and an efficient coatstand had replaced the iron hook in the wall. There hadn't been time to remove the fluorescent strip lights, but their job had been taken over by several strategically placed brass floor lamps with ivory silk shades. The window, unfortunately, was still bare, and still didn't admit much light, but Corinne had ordered rough, open-weave peach drapes, and she could visualize exactly how they would soften the appearance of the room.

She opened the suitcase and took out a framed photograph of Charlie, which she placed on her credenza. Then she carefully shook out the folds of an intricately embroidered wall hanging, worked in shades of peach and pale blue. She hammered some special hooks into the wall, then stepped back to admire the effect of the vibrant silk against the ivory wall. It was all she had hoped for.

Finally, she reached into the suitcase and drew out a blue porcelain bowl wrapped in several layers of old bath towel. She placed the bowl in the center of the coffee table and emitted another happy sigh. Once the drapes were in place and the bowl was filled with fresh flowers, her office would be perfect.

Alma Grady, Dan's secretary, poked her head around the open door. "Corinne, I managed to reach the insurance company on Friday afternoon..." Her voice tailed away into awestruck silence. "Oh, my heavens!" she murmured, her voice harsh with shock. "I can't believe what I'm seeing! How in the world did you manage to do all this in the one week Dan was away?"

Corinne sat down on her elegant new sofa, feeling all the excitement drain out of her. Dan's personal secretary was in her fifties and had been with the company from its very first day. Corinne knew her loyalty to Dan was unquestioning, but—foolishly perhaps—she had hoped Alma would recognize the many advantages that would come from cheering up the offices.

She sighed. "Alma, I'm sorry you don't like it, and I apologize if you think I took advantage of Dan's absence, but I felt I was doing something of benefit for the whole company. I simply couldn't work somewhere as gloomy as this room used to be." Her control suddenly snapped. "Darn it, Alma! It wasn't even efficient! *None* of these offices is efficiently planned! This room was huge, but there was nowhere to file papers except a rickety desk drawer that was coming loose from its moorings. If I sat down, there was nowhere for anybody else to sit, and if you walked too fast across the floor you risked tripping yourself on the holes in the linoleum."

Alma perched on the sofa opposite Corinne. "You misunderstood me," she said. "I wasn't complaining, I was just envious! I was wondering how long I'd have to wait before it was my turn. You know, when we moved into this place ten years ago it was dreary, but at least it was functional. Since then, the management group has been so caught up in improving the factory and building the new design lab that they've never noticed the office equipment is practically disintegrating under our noses. I guess I didn't really notice either, not until last week when you brought in the work crews and I realized how much I hated those horrible green walls."

Corinne laughed aloud with relief. "Alma, you've no idea how pleased I am to have your approval. There're bound to be several weeks of dust and mess, and it's good to know—"

The rest of her words were cut off by a resounding crash that echoed from the reception area all the way down the main corridor. The crash was immediately followed by a muffled roar of male outrage and the sound of rapidly approaching footsteps.

"Dan's back from Washington!" Alma sprang up from the sofa, her face a picture of guilt.

"So he is," Corinne murmured. "I wonder if he had a good time." She leaned back against the peach pillows of her sofa, feeling an odd sense of exhilaration. As she picked up one of the folders Alma had left on the coffee table and began leafing slowly through the information-packed pages, the clatter of a pail, and another anguished roar, marked Dan's progress along the corridor.

Her office door was thrown wide open. She winced as it banged against the smooth ivory wall. Doorstops, she thought. They'd have to install doorstops or the paint job would be ruined within the week.

"So you're here!" Dan bellowed. "What the hell have you been doing while I was away?"

Corinne glanced up from her folder. "Hello, Dan," she said sweetly. "Welcome back. How was Washington?"

He stormed into the room, stopping just in time to save himself from a close encounter with the edge of the coffee table. Alma murmured a few inaudible words and sidled from the room, shutting the door behind her. Dan didn't even seem to notice his secretary's departure.

He stared at Corinne with an expression of disillusionment. "You promised you wouldn't make any major decisions while I was gone," he said. "And, like a fool, I believed you."

She stood up, meeting his eyes with a level gaze of her own. "I didn't promise not to make any major decisions," she said quietly. "You said there were several important decisions pending, and I promised not to oppose you on any of those."

"That distinction is a bit too subtle for me, I'm afraid. You'll have to forgive me. Plumbing hardware is a down-to-earth business, you know, and I'm used to dealing with people who mean pretty much what you think they mean."

"Oh, come on, Dan, quit the 'I'm just a simple country boy' act! I'm sick and tired of hearing that the Dansted Corporation is a plumbing company. Guess what? Around the fifty-fifth time, I got the message."

Dan slowly inspected her office, his gaze contemptuous. "When I left for Washington, you promised you would make no important decisions in my absence. I suppose turning headquarters upside down and forbidding any of my managers to inform me of what was going on doesn't qualify as an important decision in your book."

"I gave you a promise and I kept it. Ask Warren. Ask Frank. Ask the company treasurer. I've sat in on their meetings without so much as expressing an opinion, let alone forcing them to accept my views."

"Corinne, just because you haven't voiced an opinion at a few company meetings doesn't mean you haven't made any important decisions. You knew damn well how I'd feel about your having my entire headquarters rebuilt."

"The offices are being painted, Dan, and I'm having some new flooring laid. Nobody's rebuilding anything."

"So why were those workmen tearing a hole in the ceiling over Debbie's desk?"

"They're putting in a skylight," Corinne replied, striding over to the window. Her whole purpose in redecorating the offices had been to annoy Dan, and if she wanted him to buy her out of the company—on her terms—she ought to do everything in her power to fan the flames of his irritation. Unfortunately, as Charlie had often warned her, she lacked the ability to remain emotionally distant. After only a week at Dansted Corporation headquarters, she genuinely cared about the people here. And because she cared, she discovered she wanted Dan to approve of the changes she'd instigated.

"The reception area was so dark," she explained. "I talked it over with Debbie and, as it happens, she's really a keen gardener. We decided that if we put in a skylight, there'd be enough sun even in winter to support some tall indoor plants. If it turns out that we've miscalculated, Debbie feels confident that she can cope with artificial lights."

She looked at Dan pleadingly. "The reception area

didn't do justice to the achievements of your company, Dan. Try to imagine it with clean white walls, a Mexican tiled floor, and some tropical plants for some life and color. I'm not saying you'll sell more plumbing fixtures just because the lobby looks attractive, but I'm certain you won't sell less. And I'll guarantee your work force will be more responsive."

Dan's gaze lingered for a moment on her mouth. "You don't understand the Dansted Corporation," he said, his voice oddly abstracted. "The people in this company are turned on by fine engineering, not by white paint and a lobby that looks like a miniature jungle."

"You're wrong, Dan," she said softly. "You keep forgetting how much this company's grown in the last five years. Most of your office employees aren't crusty old engineers. They're young married women who work here because the pay's good and because their families need the extra income to make their mortgage payments."

"Are you suggesting that married women with mortgages work better if they're surrounded by potted palm trees?"

She smiled, not sure why her heart had suddenly started to knock violently against her ribs. "Yes," she said. "And I think you'll be surprised at how many of your male engineers like the potted palms every bit as much as the female clerks."

Dan gave her an enigmatic glance. "Just make sure the painters never stray into my office," he said. He turned and left without saying anything more, closing the door behind him with a gentle click.

Chapter Six

OVER THE NEXT couple of weeks, Corinne's office became the unofficial meeting place for the entire company. Frank and Warren, along with Dan, stubbornly refused to allow the painters anywhere near their own gloomy offices, yet they always found some reason why it was more practical to gather in Corinne's bright, comfortable surroundings than in the dreary official conference room.

Organizing the decorators and scheduling deliveries of office furniture was demanding, but it didn't take up all of Corinne's time. The insurance industry had been one of her major areas of study in college, and she set about finding cheaper, more comprehensive group health insurance for the Dansted Corporation employees. Scott Harris, the company treasurer, was ecstatic when she explained the increased benefits she had negotiated, all of which could be bought at a thirteen percent reduction in premium. Health insurance costs were a major expense for the company, and even Dan responded to news of the changed policy with a terse compliment.

For Corinne, her first three weeks with the company were a mixed triumph. On the one hand, she was gratified by the visible boost in company morale. The Dansted Corporation had always enjoyed good management-employee relations. Now, however, there was an added note of excitement and cheerfulness. Every time she stepped out of her office, people would tell her how much they appreciated the fresh paint, or the comfort and efficiency of their new furniture. In fact, despite all the confusion and mess, productivity in the clerical department had actually increased while the redecorating was going on.

On the other hand, Corinne suspected her active involvement in company affairs was not having the desired effect on Dan. After his initial outburst, he'd had very little to say. His mouth tightened ominously every time he came across an unexpected paint bucket, but his reaction when she showed him the first bill from the furniture warehouse was unexpected. He merely glanced at the total, then looked up at her steadily.

"Have you checked the figures?"

She nodded. "They're correct." She hadn't intended to justify the staggering total, but she heard herself saying, "We bought twenty new desks and chairs, as well as four new sofas and eight credenzas. The price is actually quite reasonable for such a large order."

"Is it?" he said. "It's been a long time since I went shopping for furniture." He picked up his pen, twisting it idly between his fingers. "You know, as the majority shareholder in this company, you have a perfect right to sign this invoice without bringing it to me."

"I prefer to keep you informed," she said quietly. "I think you should know how much of the company's money I'm spending."

He scrawled his signature across the invoice. "Debbie is thrilled to bits with her new plants," he said as he handed Corinne the invoice, and she was surprised to see a faint gleam of amusement in his eyes. "I can't wait for that bill to arrive. I'm anxious to see how much that indoor jungle has cost me."

She found herself smiling. "Less than the furniture, if it's any consolation."

The painters finished work on a Friday, and she celebrated by inviting Debbie and Alma to join her at The Happy Trapper, a local seafood restaurant. They all ate lobster drenched in butter sauce, and the meal was a great success. It was only after she parted company from her colleagues that Corinne stopped to ask herself precisely what she was celebrating. With a sinking of her stomach, she realized how far she had drifted from her original goals. She wasn't supposed to be making the Dansted Corporation run more smoothly, for heaven's sake! She was supposed to be making herself an ever-present thorn in Dan's side, annoying enough so he would hurry up and agree to marry her.

The next morning Corinne woke up early, even though it was Saturday of the Fourth of July weekend, and she hadn't set her alarm. She lay in bed, trying to fall asleep again, but relaxation proved impossible. *Face facts,* she told herself gloomily. *You've been in Rhode Island for three and a half weeks and your plans are pretty much in a shambles.* Dan Matthews, unfortunately, was not conforming to any of her preconceived notions. With a touch of irritation, she ordered herself to stop thinking about him. After all, she was only interested in him as a biologically sound male who might eventually get her pregnant. Her mind spiraled off on an intriguing tangent as she imagined how attractive Dan's biologically sound body would look when stripped of its three-piece business suit.

She jumped out of bed and marched into the shower, turning the taps on full blast. By the time she'd dried herself off, her mental system seemed to be functioning a little more rationally. She walked briskly to the closet, reaching inside to find a pair of jeans. She would stop by the office for a couple of hours, she decided. Late yesterday, the posters she'd ordered from a local print shop had been delivered. Even with its new coat of cream-colored paint, the lunchroom wasn't particularly attractive, and she was anxious to see if the colorful pictures would cheer it up.

Forty-five minutes later she arrived at the factory. She had never been there on the weekend, and the empty building seemed unexpectedly dark and spooky. She hurried down the dimly lit corridor toward the lunchroom, glancing in to each office she passed, even though she knew she wasn't likely to find anyone there on a holiday weekend.

The janitor had left a small stepladder propped in a corner of the lunchroom, and the posters were stacked against the walls. Huge, bright red tomatoes and dewy peaches vied for attention with blue-green heads of broccoli and crunchy-looking carrots.

After a quick survey of the room, she opened the ladder against the middle of the wall directly opposite the windows. The posters, mounted on wallboard, were light and easy to handle, and she hummed tunelessly to herself as she banged in the first couple of hooks. She selected a picture of purple grapes nestling against green apples, clambered up the stepladder again, then leaned back to make sure she had hung it straight.

"It's too high on the left. You need to push it down a bit."

At the sound of Dan's voice, she jerked around much too fast. Her feet tangled with each other on the stepladder, and she began to fall. He stepped forward quickly to catch her, saving her from an awkward tumble onto the hard tile floor.

For a long moment she lay unmoving against him. He was wearing a casual cotton shirt unbuttoned halfway to his waist, and she could feel his chest rising and falling rapidly beneath her cheek. If she moved her hand even a little bit, she would be able to touch the dark hair revealed by his open shirt. Her throat suddenly felt constricted, and her lungs ached, as if there wasn't enough oxygen in the room.

Dan gazed down at her in total silence, and she noticed abstractedly that his cheeks were flushed and his eyes had darkened to a deep, stormy shade of gray.

"I'm sorry," he said at last, his voice sounding oddly strained. "I didn't mean to startle you."

"It's all right. No harm done, since you were there to catch me." She wondered how her voice could sound so normal when her body was slowly disintegrating. If he let go of her, she would surely shatter into a thousand pieces.

"Corinne . . ."

She swallowed hard. "Yes?"

"Stop me," he said unsteadily. "You should stop me from doing this." And he bent his head downward until his mouth touched hers in a swift, hesitant caress.

She went absolutely still. Then his arms tightened around her, and she felt her body melting into his. Her breasts were flattened against the firm plane of his chest, her hips glued to his thighs, but she didn't try to move away. His tongue stroked insistently against her lips, and she opened her mouth with a tiny gasp of astonishment. They were so close that she inevitably felt the swift hardening of his body as their kiss deepened, and she knew in that moment that she had dreamed of this kiss for weeks. She drank in the taste of him, her hips rocking instinctively as she sought ever more intimate contact with the muscled strength of his body. Somewhere in the dark blaze of excitement that enveloped her, she thought how strange it was that the thrust of his tongue inside her mouth could weaken her legs until they felt too feeble to support her.

He drew back abruptly, grasping her arms to steady her as he gazed down into her face. "This is insane," he said huskily.

"Yes." She lifted her hand and touched his mouth lightly with her forefinger.

He drew in a harsh breath, deliberately parting his lips so that her finger slipped inside his mouth. He gently bit down on it and she closed her eyes, swaying toward him in an unconscious gesture of surrender.

This time there was nothing hesitant about his kiss. His hands were commanding as they positioned her against his body. His hot mouth tasted of passion. Dizzy with new sensations, she clenched her hands in the thickness of his hair, responding without any thought except how right it felt to be held in his arms. Her mind was a void, floating in space, but her body was a small flame, waiting for the larger fire that would consume her.

Once again, it was Dan who broke their embrace, pushing her away quite suddenly, his grip on her arms tight enough to make her wince. She took a few steps backward, scarcely aware of what she was doing, although she was feverishly—achingly—aware of what he had done to her.

"Corinne, I'm sorry." His voice sounded amazingly controlled, and she looked up quickly, wondering if she had misinterpreted the previous intensity of his arousal. Heaven knew she was hardly an expert in assessing such things.

"You have extremely tempting lips," he said, giving her a small, rueful smile. "But you don't have to tell me that's no excuse for falling on you like a high-school kid in mating season."

"When I was in high school, mating season lasted twelve months a year. Don't let's make one small kiss into a big issue, Dan." She couldn't believe that the cool, faintly amused voice was her own. Her heart was still pounding, and her nipples felt tight and hard beneath her concealing bra, but hell could freeze over before she would let Dan know how he'd affected her. His body showed no sign of continuing arousal and, apart from a faint glitter in his eyes, his expression betrayed no hint of carefully leashed passion. Although, of course, the dismal truth was that she hadn't the faintest idea what carefully leashed passion actually looked like.

"Thanks, Corinne, I appreciate your understanding." Dan obviously thought they had said everything that needed to be said on the subject. Maybe they had. "These are wonderful posters," he remarked offhandedly. "Would you like some help hanging them?"

She pushed her hands into the pockets of her jeans and did her best to match his casual tone. "Yes, please. I always have trouble getting pictures to sit square on the wall."

"The secret is that you have to measure," he said. "I have a measuring tape and a carpenter's level in my office. If you wait a minute, I'll get them."

As soon as he left the room, she sank down into a chair, disturbingly aware that something important had happened when Dan kissed her. Their conversation during the last couple of minutes could hardly have been more mundane, yet the electricity coursing through her body belied the impersonal words.

Dan returned with an impressive collection of tools,

and she jumped up from the chair, doing her best to look brisk and efficient. He smiled at her. "Do you want all the posters hung on this wall here?" he asked.

"I think so, don't you?" She discovered that if she didn't look at him, she could manage to keep her heart beating at a nearly normal rate. She blew a wisp of hair out of her eyes and silently thanked heaven she hadn't made a total ass of herself by blurting out something that probably wasn't even true. Dan's kiss had only seemed so shattering because nobody had ever kissed her that way before. Good grief, she still wasn't sure she even *liked* the wretched man."

She picked up a couple of posters and placed them side by side against the wall. "What do you think? Is this a good place for them?"

"Looks good to me." Dan spoke around a mouthful of picture hooks.

Hanging the twelve posters took almost two hours, far longer than Corinne had expected. "They're very effective," he said as they both stepped back to admire them. "This room needed some bright colors, and this wall is too large to be left bare."

"To be honest, I was trying a bit of subtle propaganda. I found out from the cook that the most frequently ordered item on the menu is doughnuts, followed closely by french fries and pastries. I thought that with all the summer fruits coming into season, these posters might encourage a few of the men to occasionally eat a fresh peach instead of a peach-flavored Danish."

"A nutritionist as well as an interior designer?" he teased. "You're a multitalented woman, Corinne."

"Business courses have changed quite a lot in the last couple of years," she said. "Several of my professors stressed the importance of good health and pleasant surroundings if employees are to work efficiently."

Dan tossed a couple of bent nails into the garbage and concentrated on rewinding his measuring tape. "I'm not the world's best at admitting that I was wrong, Corinne, particularly when I have to keep admitting it to the same person. But I made a mistake when I allowed the company's offices to get so run-down! You were absolutely right to insist on bringing in painters and ordering new furniture. I should have done it at least four years ago, as soon as we had the money to spare."

When Dan decided to make an apology, he did it generously, and Corinne felt her cheeks grow warm with pleasure. "I admire the way you run the company, Dan, and it's important to me to know you approve of what I've done," she said quietly. Then her eyes sparkled provocatively. "But now we get to the really important question: Are you going to call back the workmen so they can redecorate *your* office?"

He grinned. "Sure, why not? Since I'm admitting I was wrong, why not go whole hog and admit I've been dying to ask for your help in selecting some new furniture. I get jealous every time I see you working at your desk. I draw the line at pink curtains, though."

"I'll select something suitably dignified and masculine," she promised. "How about beige and brown in your office, since we have beige and peach in mine?"

"Sounds ominously sexist," he said. "The Equal Opportunity Office will arrest us if you're not careful."

She laughed. "Seriously, Dan, I have some furniture catalogs and some color charts in my office, if you'd like to look at them."

She was aware of a fractional hesitation before he said, "I have a better idea. Do you have any special plans for this afternoon?"

She gave a totally unnecessary twitch to one of the posters before replying. "No," she said finally. "Nothing that can't be postponed."

"Then how about coming back to my apartment? It's just across the border in Connecticut. I was going to pick up some fried chicken on my way home and eat it out on the terrace. We could discuss color schemes and furniture styles during the drive."

Some instinct warned her that it would be wiser not to go. Another more primitive one prompted her to accept. Primitiveness won out. "An invitation to an almost-picnic on the Fourth of July weekend," she said lightly. "How can I resist?"

It was noon when they arrived in Putnam, the small town closest to Dan's apartment. They bought nine pieces of extra-crunchy chicken and a pound of potato salad, and then Dan insisted on stopping at the local ice-cream parlor for a tub of chocolate-coconut ice cream. Corinne briefly wondered how many days she'd have to live on cottage cheese and celery sticks to make up for such reckless indulgence, then decided she didn't care.

"It's only about ten minutes from here to my apartment," Dan said as they returned to his Mazda RX–7, depositing the various boxes on the back seat of the car. "So are we agreed on my office color scheme?"

"I think so. Ivory walls, the same beige carpet as mine, teamed with beige drapes, and a dark brown tweedy sofa."

"And the biggest desk in the Habco catalog."

"I'll order it on Tuesday," she agreed. "We've just about bought out their warehouse stock, so it may take a few weeks to arrive."

"I guess I'll have to be patient, which isn't one of my

stronger suits." He pointed to a small but obviously luxurious apartment complex set well back from the road
and surrounding a tree-shaded courtyard. "That's where
I live," he said. "Mary Beth wanted to keep our house,
so I moved here when we filed for divorce. There's a
swimming pool in the back, and the maintenance company does a good job with the gardens. I've found it
very comfortable."

"It looks great," Corinne said.

He drew the car to a halt in the underground parking
garage. "You grab the ice cream, and I'll take the chicken,"
he said. "The elevator's right over there, and I live on
the top floor."

His apartment was spacious, which she had expected,
and furnished mainly with antiques, which she found
surprising. "Did you buy the furniture yourself?" she
asked as she followed him into the luxuriously appointed
kitchen.

"A few pieces. But most of the really good stuff was
a gift from my mother. She loves to browse around antique shops, whereas I've never really had the time or
inclination. When you travel overseas as much as I do,
it cuts into your weekends pretty drastically." He opened
the freezer door. "You can put the ice cream in here,"
he said. "I don't think we need to heat up the chicken,
do you?"

"Oh no! All the best picnic chicken is served luke-
warm."

He took a jug of lemonade from the fridge and arranged glasses, paper plates, napkins, and cutlery on a
large wooden tray and picked it up. "Could you carry
the food?" he asked. "The terrace is right off the living
room. Follow me."

The southern wall of Dan's living room was virtually

all glass, and an oversized sliding door opened onto a huge, flower-bedecked terrace. "The view was basically what tempted me to buy this apartment," he said. "The terrace overlooks a small wood, and I think you'll enjoy eating out here."

Corinne gasped with pleasure. "Dan, it's beautiful. Not quite as beautiful as the Rocky Mountains, of course, but a pretty good runner-up for the East Coast!"

He set the tray on a glass-topped, wrought-iron table. "Watch your tongue, lady, particularly today. Remember it's we Yankees who fought and died to provide you western cowpokes with a Fourth of July holiday."

Grinning, she opened the cartons of food, and he deftly piled potato salad and chicken onto two paper plates, handing one to her with a flourish. Corinne suddenly discovered that she was ravenous. She ate a breast and almost all of the potato salad before leaning back in her lounge chair, taking small bites from a crispy drumstick and chewing contentedly.

"This time last year I was in England," Dan remarked. "The American Embassy threw a huge party, and I was invited, but somehow a manicured English lawn isn't quite the right place for cherry pie and fireworks."

Corinne found herself remembering her own previous Fourth of July celebration. She and Charlie had driven into the mountains. While he fished in the South Platte River, she had stretched out beside him on a sun-drenched rock. Later, when the sun went down, they'd cooked the freshly caught fish over a smoky wood fire. The image was so vivid that a piercing wave of nostalgia engulfed her.

She sat up, swallowing over the sudden lump in her throat. "This was Charlie's all-time favorite meal," she said, gesturing to the box of chicken. "He used to complain more about having to give up fried chicken than he did about not being allowed to smoke or drink."

Dan looked up sharply. "What do you mean? Charlie hadn't given up smoking—*or* drinking, for that matter! My uncle could drink most men under the table, and he smoked a cigar every time we had dinner together."

"Did he?" Corinne smiled wistfully. "He wasn't supposed to, of course, but I'm not surprised. He always came back from those New York visits looking like the tomcat who's swallowed the pet canary—a little bit guilty but blissfully content."

"My uncle died of a coronary," Dan said. "Are you saying that he *knew* he had a heart condition? Is that why he wasn't supposed to drink or smoke?"

Corinne stirred a sprig of mint around in her glass of lemonade. "Yes," she said finally. "Charlie knew he had a heart condition—and dangerously high blood pressure. He'd known it for several years. In fact, he lived much longer than any of his doctors predicted."

"In God's name, why didn't he tell me? Why didn't he tell anybody in his family?"

"He didn't want you to know he was dying. I thought he should confide in you, but he wouldn't. I kept hoping you'd notice something was wrong and force him to discuss the situation honestly, but you never did. I guess he managed to put on a convincing act for the few hours a month you two were together. It isn't as if you ever spent much time with him."

Dan put down his plate and drew in a deep breath. "Corinne, I think maybe we should clear up a few misunderstandings. First of all, it wasn't me who cut down on the frequency of our meetings; it was Charlie. From the time he married you, my uncle no longer seemed interested in having me visit him in Denver. He got pretty wrapped up in building that new house for you, and whenever I would suggest flying out for a weekend of fishing or skiing he'd come up with a dozen different reasons why it would be better if I waited. By the time your house was finished, my marriage to Mary Beth was in a state of terminal sickness, and I wasn't being very sociable with anybody. Later, when I got my act together again, I realized that Charlie's attitude toward me had permanently changed. He made it plain that he didn't want me intruding into your married life and, naturally, I accepted his wishes."

"I guess it's my turn to apologize," Corinne said with new insight. "I should have realized he was deliberately keeping us apart. He always praised you to the skies, and yet—from my perspective—you seemed utterly indifferent to his welfare. The truth is that he was obsessed with not worrying you or your family about his health. He often said he'd seen the way people react when close relatives are dying, and he didn't want any part of that miserable scene. I guess he thought it would be easier to conceal the real state of his health if he only met you in a dark restaurant. It wouldn't have been possible for him to keep up the act for an entire weekend. He was taking a lot of medication, and he sometimes found it so difficult to breathe that we kept a supply of oxygen in his bedroom."

"It must have been incredibly tough for you," Dan said softly. "How long were you married before you found out Charlie was sick?"

Corinne stood up and walked across the terrace. She stared unseeingly at the distant trees for a long time before turning around and leaning against the white iron balustrade.

"I knew Charlie was sick when I married him," she

said. "In fact, neither of us expected him to live much more than a few months after the wedding. The only reason we married was because we both thought he was dying."

Dan came and stood beside her, taking care to leave several inches of space between them. "I've already jumped to far too many wrong conclusions where you're concerned," he said quietly. "So would you mind telling me why you married my uncle, knowing he was so sick?"

She lifted her chin proudly. "I've told you before. It was a marriage of convenience. I married your uncle for his money."

"Maybe you did," Dan said, his voice unexpectedly gentle, "but I think that's only a small part of the story, and I'd like to hear the rest."

Corinne was worried by how much she wanted Dan to know the truth. Why was it so important, when she had never felt the slightest need to enlighten anybody else? She rubbed her arms, which suddenly felt chilled despite the hot summer sun.

"Corinne," Dan said quietly, "how did you and my uncle first meet?"

"I was eighteen years old," she said, avoiding his eyes. "I worked in a bar on Colfax Avenue, definitely not the best part of Denver. I had left home when I was sixteen, and I'd worked there ever since. It was illegal to employ me, of course, but I faked my ID, and the owner wasn't interested in inspecting it too closely. He paid me less than the minimum wage, but the tips were okay, and neither of us paid any income tax. He had no incentive to fire me, and I had no incentive to quit."

"You dropped out of high school to run away to Denver?"

She tried to keep the harshness out of her voice, without quite succeeding. "I quit high school after my soph-omore year," she said. "My mother was ... ill ... and needed somebody home with her all the time. She died just after I turned sixteen."

"I'm sorry. That's very young to lose a parent."

"She'd been sick for quite a while," Corinne replied briefly. She had never discussed with anybody the al-coholic stupor in which her mother spent the last months of her life, and she wasn't about to do so now. Thankfully, Dan didn't pursue the subject.

"Why didn't you reenroll in school?" he asked.

She shrugged. "Chiefly to annoy my father, I think. I spent the best part of the next six months stuck in front of the television set, watching game shows. That's when I wasn't racing around town on the back of some boy's motorcycle, or scrawling graffiti on the police-station wall."

"What made you decide to move to Denver?"

She shifted restlessly against the railing. "My father and I had a fight. He was one of those parents who thought that sparing the rod spoiled the child, and one day I got tired of the hassle."

Dan waited, obviously sensing what a great deal she had left unsaid, but she had no intention of mentioning the endless beatings her father had inflicted on her in the name of "discipline" and "obedience."

"Is your father still alive?" he asked eventually.

"Yes. I've seen him a couple of times since I got married. Charlie made me invite him for a visit soon after I started college. Dad brought his new wife with him, and they seemed genuinely fond of each other. You would never have known how cruel he'd been. If you could have seen him with my mother when they were having one of their fights—" Her voice broke embarrassingly and she turned away, struggling to control the painful memories.

Dan didn't say anything. He walked over to the table and picked up their two glasses of lemonade. "Here," he said, handing her one. He waited until she'd taken a few sips, then said casually, "I guess you met my uncle when he came into the bar where you worked?"

"Yes." She was grateful for the tactful change of subject. The lemonade was tart and cool, and the memories of her parents sank back into the distant reaches of her mind where she usually kept them.

"Was Charlie a regular customer at your bar? I know he always enjoyed Denver's night life."

Just thinking about her first meeting with Charlie made Corinne's lips curve into a tender smile. "No, he only came into the bar that one time. He wasn't drunk when he arrived, although I could tell he'd already been drinking for a good while. I kept an eye on him because it was part of my job to warn the bouncer when I spotted a drunk who was likely to cause trouble. But Charlie was one of those rare people who simply become kinder and more cheerful as they drink, so I didn't mind serving him at all. Besides, he gave me a five-dollar tip every time I brought him a beer, and as far as I was concerned, that made him a really terrific guy."

"Did you always rate men strictly according to how well they tipped?"

There was no hint of condemnation in Dan's voice, merely curiosity, and she answered honestly. "No. Basically I rated men and women according to how they behaved when they were drunk. Charlie was one of the nicest drunks I'd ever encountered, and five-dollar tips weren't common in that particular bar, so he won out on two counts. When I brought him his sixth beer, he doubled his tip, which meant I'd made thirty-five bucks in a couple of hours. On my budget, thirty-five dollars wasn't something to be sneezed at, so after a while I went back over to see if he wanted to order anything else. He was passed out cold, and when I shifted him around a little, I could see he'd banged his head on the edge of the table. He was already growing a lump as big as a golf ball right in the middle of his forehead. The owner checked Charlie's wallet, but he didn't have any credit cards with his address, so we couldn't put him in a cab and send him home. For some reason, maybe because I felt I owed him something for all those tips, I volunteered to take him back to my apartment."

"That was a pretty risky move on your part."

Corinne regarded him steadily. "He wasn't the first person I'd taken home," she said. "And if you'd known me in those days, Dan, you wouldn't have been so worried. Between the motorcycle gang back in Grand Junction and the bar on Colfax, I'd been around a whole bunch of places where a young woman doesn't usually go. I was eighteen, but unless you peered very intently under the layers of makeup, I looked every day of a hardliving thirty. I guess there were a few things I hadn't seen, but offhand I can't imagine what they were."

"Once you got him home, did he give you a rough night?" Dan asked sympathetically.

"On the contrary. He didn't wake up until late the next morning. When he finally stopped moaning and groaning for a few seconds, I told him to stop making such a fuss and haul his tail into the shower. 'You're not dying,' I said. 'You're just hung over. Coffee's perking, and the aspirin's in the medicine chest.' He laughed then, and told me I was wrong. He *was* dying. The reason he'd gotten so drunk was because the foremost specialist in Colorado had just informed him he had dangerously high blood pressure and an inoperable heart condition. The specialist gave him two months to live."

She saw Dan's knuckles whiten around the glass. "Dammit, Corinne! You're telling me that Charlie was warned about the state of his health more than seven years ago! How could he have been sick all those years without ever telling his family? And don't feed me that crap about not wanting to worry us. If he'd trusted me, if he'd really cared about our relationship, he'd have wanted me to know."

Instinctively she reached out to console him, laying her hand on his arm. When she felt his hard muscles tighten beneath her fingers, she hastily removed her hand. "Dan, don't think that way," she said urgently. "Look at it from Charlie's point of view. He believed he had only a couple of months left to enjoy himself. He hadn't a money worry in the world. He wasn't facing major surgery, so he didn't need your moral support. All he wanted was for his remaining few weeks with you and your family to be comfortable and easy. He didn't want to ruin your last meetings with sad stories and mournful reminiscences."

"Maybe," Dan agreed reluctantly. "But he trusted you. He took you into his confidence, even though you were a total stranger."

"Dan, surely you can see that's exactly why he confided in me. He was scared, and he wanted to express his fears to somebody who wasn't emotionally involved. Charlie had an instinct for understanding people. He probably took one look at me and realized I was so tough that one unknown old man dying wouldn't even make a ripple in my life."

"I'd be willing to bet you were never as stony hearted

as you're trying to make out."

"Then you'd lose," she said abruptly. "Anyway, it turned out that the doctors had ordered Charlie to hire a live-in nurse. He didn't want to do that, so he compromised by offering me a job as his housekeeper."

"I'm surprised you took it," Dan said. "If half of what you've said about yourself is true, taking care of a sick, elderly man hardly seems your style."

"As I said before, your uncle had a genius for understanding people," Corinne said, smiling as she visualized Charlie pacing the tiny floor of her living room, groaning with the aftereffects of his hangover. "He figured out immediately that I'd be delighted to work for him provided he offered enough money. He asked me how much I earned at the bar each week, including tips, then offered me double to become his housekeeper. I bargained a bit, suggesting he pay the rent on my apartment so I'd have somewhere to come back to after he died. He agreed, and that was that. He went to take a shower, and I threw a few clothes into a duffle bag. Then we had coffee and drove over to his house in Cherry Hills. I never moved back into that apartment."

"I have the feeling you're making a complex story sound far too simple. If my uncle was diagnosed as being terminally ill, how did he manage to live for another seven years? I don't understand what happened."

"Neither did his doctors," Corinne said with a wry smile. "The heart specialist said that ninety percent of Charlie's problems were originally brought on by his lifestyle. For years he ate nothing but junk food, never exercised, smoked like a chimney, and drank too much."

"I always thought it was the cigars and the rich food that made life worth living for Charlie."

"It's amazing how your perspective can change when

the doctor hands you a death sentence," Corinne said. "Charlie wasn't ready to die, and he was willing to make some changes. As it happened, because of all those months I'd spent nursing my mother, I knew something about basic nutrition. And when teenagers decide to do something, they tend to do it with a great deal of enthusiasm. I suddenly decided that Charlie and I were going on a health kick—with a vengeance! I locked up the alcohol and persuaded him to quit smoking, and we both started eating three small meals regularly each day—fruit, fish, and whole grain cereals instead of pizza, cheeseburgers, and fried chicken. Charlie must have had the basic constitution of an ox, because we woke up one morning and realized that three months had passed and he wasn't dead. On the contrary, he was feeling more energetic than he had in years. We trotted back to the specialists, and they said his blood pressure was down but his heart condition was unchanged. They congratulated him and said he just might make it through another six months if he was careful."

"How long ago was that?" Dan asked.

"Six and a half years," she said with a tiny smile. "When he heard he had another six months left, he somehow convinced me I wanted to enroll in college. He paid a special tutor to prepare me for the high-school equivalency diploma, and on the day I heard I'd passed, he offered to pay my tuition fees at the University of Denver. He said I'd given him the gift of six months extra life, so the least he could do was to give me the gift of an education."

Dan reached up and touched the wetness at the corners of her eyes. "That's when he asked you to marry him?" he said softly.

The gentle touch of his hands against her face made

Corinne feel cared for in a way she had never before experienced. With considerable difficulty, she resisted the impulse to throw herself into his arms and cry endless tears against the comforting strength of his shoulder. She felt vulnerable to his warmth and was terrified by the feeling. Ever since she had watched her mother drink herself to death, Corinne had sworn she would never again allow her emotions to be held hostage by another person. Charlie had shown her that there were caring, generous people in the world and she had grown to love him, but she knew instinctively that she would be risking something entirely new if she allowed herself to form any serious emotional tie to Dan Matthews.

Pulling away from him, she walked back to the table and began scraping chicken bones into an empty carton. "Charlie wanted to be sure I'd have enough money to complete my education," she said. "He could have set up a trust fund, but he decided it would be easier to marry me. That way, nobody could dispute my right to inherit his money. We got married on my nineteenth birthday."

Dan's smile was full of affectionate warmth. "So good old Uncle Charlie fooled all the doctors right up to the end! I'll bet that must have pleased him."

"Yes, although after a while his doctors became fascinated by his determination to survive. The heart specialist actually became a good friend of ours. He's writing a paper about the case, you know. He told me once that it's lucky most of his diagnoses are more accurate than the one he gave Charlie, or he'd be out of business."

She heard Dan crossing the terrace. He came to a halt just behind her, so close that she could feel the warmth of his breath against the back of her neck. Her stomach gave the uncomfortable little lurch his proximity always seemed to precipitate. He touched her lightly on the shoulder, and she moved quickly to one side.

"Sorry," she said with false joviality. "Was I in your way?"

His eyes glinted silver. "Not exactly," he replied. He tucked a loose wisp of hair carefully behind her ear, then leaned over the table to close the lid on the remains of the potato salad. He tossed a crumpled napkin onto the tray and smiled up at her with complete naturalness.

"Ready for dessert? he asked. He sounded so relaxed that Corinne decided she must have imagined that moment of threatening, electrical tension between them. He patted his flat stomach. "Despite all you've told me about the virtues of steamed fish, my degenerate soul is still craving chocolate-coconut ice cream. Do you think we could eat a couple of small scoops?"

She hadn't realized she'd been holding her breath. She exhaled it quickly, then managed to return his smile. "*I* sure could," she said. "In fact, I could probably eat a couple of *large* scoops."

"A sinner after my own heart," he said as they carried the remains of their picnic into the kitchen. "Can I make you some coffee? That's my one claim to culinary fame. I have a special grinder that my eldest sister gave me for my birthday, and I buy fancy beans from the gourmet shop in Norwich." He opened a cupboard and pointed to an array of small canisters. "You can have it flavored with orange liqueur, cinnamon, or Dutch chocolate."

"Dutch chocolate," she said promptly. "Let's go for broke."

She studied him intently as he scooped beans into the grinder. The sun had lightened a streak of his hair into a dark golden slash, and his arms were tanned to a rich mahogany. Obviously he didn't spend all his leisure time cooped up over the company account books. She wondered what he did when he wanted to relax—and who he did it with.

The ring of the doorbell interrupted a series of images that were rapidly becoming too vivid for comfort. "Shall I get that?" she asked brightly. "We wouldn't want anything to come between you and your gourmet coffeepot."

He grinned. "Wait till you taste my brew before you make sarcastic remarks about it."

The bell rang again. "Okay, I'm coming," Corinne called out. She hurried down the hallway and looked through the peephole. A young woman clad in skin-tight shorts and a miniscule halter top stood on the doorstep. Corinne opened the door.

"Hi there!" The young woman smiled, displaying twenty-eight dazzlingly white teeth. "I'm Suzanne, and I live in the apartment below this one. Is Dan home?"

"Sure am," he said before Corinne could reply. "Hello, Suzie, love. How are you?"

"Terrific, now I've seen you." She launched herself into his arms, and he gathered her close, patting her hips with careless, friendly intimacy. She raised her face expectantly, and he kissed her with brief, but thorough, intensity. Finding herself staring as his mouth pressed against Suzanne's moist, pink lips, Corinne hurriedly transferred her gaze to the wall.

"Where've you been hiding yourself?" Dan asked. "I've missed you on our morning runs. I haven't seen you for a couple of months at least."

"I was working on a project in Australia," Suzanne replied. "A new hospital, in fact. You were in China when I left."

"Well, it's great to have you back." Dan turned easily toward Corinne. "Have you two introduced yourselves? This is Suzanne McNally, who works for Hartford's most prestigious architectural firm. Suzanne, this is Corinne Steddon. She's my partner's widow, and she recently moved from Colorado to work with me at the Dansted Corporation."

"How nice for you both," Suzanne said with a friendly smile. "How are you enjoying the plumbing business?"

Corinne got as far as opening her mouth to reply before Suzanne spoke again. "Dan, is that some of your heavenly coffee I smell perking? Can I invite myself to stay for a cup?"

He smiled. "Any woman who calls my coffee heavenly is welcome to stay as long as she wants. Corinne and I were just going to eat dessert. Can I tempt you with some chocolate-coconut ice cream?"

Suzanne stroked the taut golden skin between her halter and shorts and sighed prettily. "Provided you promise to run an extra mile with me tomorrow morning," she said.

"It's a deal. You can tell me all about Australia. Do you know, I've never been there? Were you in Sydney? That's a city I've always wanted to see."

Suzanne clung to Dan's arm as he walked into the kitchen, and Corinne trailed in their wake, feeling more invisible with each passing moment. Her fair skin didn't tan easily, and she knew she must look pale and overblown beside Suzanne's lithe bronze body. Suddenly she felt scruffy and hot in her faded jeans and baggy T-shirt.

Suzanne kept up a stream of witty anecdotes about life Down Under as Dan carried the tray of coffee and dessert outside. Then, with the ease of long familiarity, she coiled herself against the cushions of a lounge chair. "I always envy you this terrace, Dan," she said. "Isn't the view marvelous, Corinne?"

"Marvelous," she agreed dryly, then felt annoyed with

herself for behaving so gauchely. "Do you have a similar balcony?" she asked politely.

"No, unfortunately not. My place is much smaller." Suzanne took a mouthful of ice cream. "Mmm . . . this is heavenly, but I mustn't forget why I came up here. I'm having a party tonight, Dan, and everybody's invited. Will you come?" She turned and smiled sweetly at Corinne. "You're invited, too, of course."

Corinne replied without stopping to think. "Thank you for the invitation, but I have another date this evening. In fact, Dan, as soon as we've finished eating, I really ought to get back to the motel."

His gaze was steady and hard. "I thought you said you didn't have any special plans today."

Suzanne was eyeing them both speculatively, and Corinne felt her cheeks grow warm. "That was for this afternoon," she said. "I have a dinner date at seven-thirty this evening." She'd always been a hopeless liar, and she could feel her cheeks flaming as she made her excuse.

Dan leaned back in his seat, but his gray eyes continued to rake her with unnerving thoroughness. "I'm sorry you can't stay," he said finally. "Suzie's parties are always occasions to remember." He turned to Suzanne. "Thanks for the invitation. I'd love to come."

"Glad you can make it." Suzanne's teeth were once again in shining evidence as she smiled radiantly at Dan. She leaned forward to pick up her coffee cup. If she moved half an inch farther, Corinne thought, nobody could even pretend that the scanty halter top was covering her nipples. Corinne put her own coffee cup back on its saucer with a decided thump.

She was piling dessert dishes into the sink when Dan came back from a prolonged farewell with Suzanne at the front door. "We'd better leave now if you have a seven-thirty appointment," he said evenly.

"Yes, of course." She carefully avoided looking at his mouth, although Suzanne hadn't been wearing lipstick, so she wasn't quite sure what proof of their kisses she expected to see. "I really enjoyed our lunch together, Dan, and I hope you have a marvelous time with Suzanne tonight."

"I'm sure I will. She's a very safe and predictable young woman."

Safe wasn't exactly the word Corinne would have used to describe Suzanne McNally. However, she was scarcely in a position to dispute Dan's judgment. They left the apartment almost immediately, and Dan kept the conversation to a series of neutral topics as they drove back to Rhode Island.

Corinne's mind was fully occupied in wrestling with what was going to happen when she and Dan parted company. Would he kiss her? Did she even want him to? She probably wouldn't compare favorably with an expert kisser like Suzanne McNally. Besides, she decided virtuously, she disliked the modern habit of bestowing open-mouthed kisses as casually as handshakes.

Dan drew the Mazda to a smooth halt in the motel parking lot. "Thanks again for a wonderful afternoon," she said as soon as he cut the engine. "I'm glad we had this opportunity to . . . talk."

"So am I." He crooked his finger under her chin and drew her face slowly around until she was forced to look at him. His thumbs moved caressingly over her cheeks as his head slowly descended.

She closed her eyes, breathless with either dread or anticipation at the prospect of his kiss. His mouth brushed with feather lightness against her lips and then her forehead. She was dazed when she felt him move away.

"I'll see you on Tuesday," he said softly. He got out of the car and politely opened the door for her. "Have a good weekend, Corinne."

"You, too," she said, and hurried into the motel lobby.

Chapter Seven

CORINNE HADN'T EVEN taken off her jacket when Alma Grady came into her office on Tuesday morning.

"Hi, Corinne, how was your weekend?"

"Great, thanks." She forced a smile. "How was yours?"

"My grandchildren came over for a picnic yesterday, and the two-year-old poured ketchup all over our poodle, the three-year-old ate so many hot dogs that he spent all night throwing up, and one set of twins climbed up our thirty-year-old oak tree to see if they could get down again. They couldn't, and we had to call the fire brigade. I guess you could say we had a marvelous time."

Corinne laughed. "How many grandchildren do you have, Alma?"

"Seven. My husband and I only have two children, but my son and his wife produced two sets of identical twins. Fortunately, they're all in school now, otherwise I don't know how my poor daughter-in-law would survive. The birth of her second set of twins gave her four children under three to take care of."

Corinne winced sympathetically. "Good grief, that's a horror that defies the imagination. Toddlers definitely need to be taken in small doses." She suddenly noticed that Dan's secretary was holding a file with a red tag attached. "Do you have something urgent for me to read, Alma?"

"Yes, the boss asked me to give you this. It's the details of our negotiations with a Mexican company called Volta Lineas. We've been discussing the possibility of setting up a joint venture with them in Tampico, Mexico. Dan has called a management group meeting in the conference room for ten o'clock. There's been an unexpected crisis in the negotiations, and he was in here working all day yesterday."

"Thanks," Corinne said, settling down at her desk and opening the file. "Let me know what you think of the posters in the lunchroom when you have a chance."

"Sure will." Alma left the room, and Corinne started reading. At five minutes before ten, she walked down the corridor to the conference room. Scott, the company treasurer, was already there talking to Warren and Frank, and Dan walked in only a few seconds after she'd taken her place at the oval table.

As always, Dan was impeccably dressed, but he looked tired. There were lines of fatigue around his eyes, and his mouth was held taut in a way she had begun to realize indicated acute inner tension. She quelled her instinctive feeling of sympathy. No doubt Suzie had given him an exhausting couple of nights, she decided caustically. Feeling Dan's gaze rest on her, she looked up. Something gleamed momentarily in his eyes, so briefly that she couldn't tell whether it was irritation or some other emotion. She quickly dropped her gaze, staring determinedly at her pencil.

Dan opened his file of papers. "Good morning," he said. "Hope you all had a good Fourth of July. I'm sorry we have to start the week off with a crisis, but I received some bad news on Sunday. Fernando Diaz, the owner of Volta Lineas, was killed in a car crash last week. He's left a widow and three daughters who haven't the faintest idea how to run a business, and they want to sell out as quickly as possible. They already have an offer from a local Mexican company, and they want a counteroffer from us within forty-eight hours."

Scott clicked his tongue disapprovingly. "That's a ridiculously short lead time, but fortunately we finished all the cost analyses on the deal over a week ago. If we decide to go ahead, it shouldn't be difficult to come up with a realistic purchase price."

"And the exchange rate is working in our favor at the moment," Dan said. "Inflation in Mexico is so bad that Mrs. Diaz would be prepared to take a lower offer in order to get her hands on some solid American dollars."

"Would the Mexican workers accept an American manager?" Corinne asked.

"They'd have to," Frank said, a touch impatiently. "With Diaz gone, we couldn't risk the deal without one of our people running the factory."

Dan outlined a couple of operational problems that needed to be considered, and the men fell into a heavily technical discussion. Corinne listened with less than half her attention, feeling the germ of an idea begin to take shape at the back of her mind. With a growing excitement, she realized that this might be the opportunity she had been waiting for.

"Please explain something to me, Dan," she said when there was a break in the discussion. "As I understand the documents in the file you gave me to read, the Mexican government won't let foreign companies take over control of local operations. We'd only be allowed to purchase less than half the shares in any company we set up with Volta Lineas. Have I understood the situation correctly?"

"Yes, you have," Dan said. "The Mexicans won't allow us to own more than forty-nine percent of the shares in any joint-venture company we might form with Volta Lineas."

"That seems a very dangerous situation for the Dansted Corporation," she said, deliberately reminding him of his own position as minority stockholder. "After all, the person who owns the majority of the shares can always do what he or she wants."

Understanding the subtle threat immediately, he whipped around to look at her, his eyes gleaming with a wintry gray light. "That's true—technically. But you're mistaken in your assumptions, Corinne. After you've been with us for a while, you'll understand that the practicalities of a business situation are quite often different from the theory. In theory, we might be helpless to control our Mexican partners. In practice, our company owns patents and technology that Volta Lineas badly wants, so it wouldn't be in their best interests to frustrate our wishes. They want the right to use our brand names in Mexico, and they know we'll pull out of the agreement if they don't run things our way. In fact, practically speaking, control would rest securely in our hands."

Frank seemed to sense an underlying tension that was out of proportion to the subject being discussed, because he broke in soothingly. "Don't worry, Corinne. There are legal ways to set up the initial agreements so that Dansted will have a considerable degree of protection under both American and Mexican laws."

"It's true we can do a lot with the legal setup," Warren said. "But I think we're underestimating the difficulties ahead of us. I visited the factory in Tampico, and nobody there, except Fernando Diaz, had the faintest concept of how to run a company efficiently. Most of his junior managers were cousins or friends he'd employed because they needed a job. His quality-control inspector has a degree in anthropology, for heaven's sake!"

The discussion raged until lunchtime, with Warren raising continuous objections to the proposed deal. From previous meetings, Corinne had already learned that he was an excessively cautious manager, and in normal circumstances she wouldn't have taken his doubts too seriously. She'd have cast her vote with Dan, whose track record in international dealings showed he had outstanding, almost intuitive grasp of foreign business ventures.

These circumstances, however, were far from normal. This was precisely the chance she had been waiting for, and she meant to take full advantage of it. She had the uneasy suspicion that if she didn't remind Dan of her proposal soon, she might well lose her nerve forever. Oddly enough, it had been easier to proposition Dan Matthews the virtual stranger than it was to repeat that proposition to Dan Matthews, the man she had begun to know and admire.

Her inner tension grew as Dan patiently summed up the advantages of the joint-venture agreement. Warren began to look reassured as Dan pointed out that Volta Lineas wouldn't be too expensive to buy into, so that even if the project failed, the Dansted Corporation could absorb the loss without significant strain. Dan really was extremely effective as the company's president, Corinne reflected, and he handled his senior managers with care and sensitivity. She was sorry she had to oppose him, and even sorrier to know she'd be running the risk of destroying the tentative friendship that had begun to grow between them.

He finished his summation and took a sip of water. "Are there any final points anybody would like to raise? ... Then do I take it I have your agreement to telephone an offer to Mrs. Diaz's lawyers this afternoon?"

As the three men nodded, Corinne cleared her throat. "I have a couple of points I'd like to discuss with you, Dan, but there's no need to keep everybody else back from lunch."

Nothing in her voice could possibly have indicated what she had in mind, yet she saw the immediate tension in the lines of his body. "We'll go into my office," he said curtly. "Gentlemen, if you'll please excuse us."

He strode down the corridor to his office, shutting the door behind them. He walked in silence to his desk, then swung around, his eyes raking her coldly. "Well, Corinne?"

With a distinct effort, she suppressed the onset of an acute attack of panic. "I'm not going to vote in favor of the Mexican joint-venture agreement," she said. Her voice, far from sounding cool and determined, sounded distinctly squeaky.

"I see," he replied after a long pause. When he spoke again, his voice deepened ironically. "I suppose you're basing that decision on years of hard-won experience in negotiating international business deals."

"No," she said. "I'm basing my decision on the fact that it's foolish for the Dansted Corporation to invest hundreds of thousands of dollars in a project where the Mexican government insists on giving somebody else legal control." She met his gaze defiantly. "As you should know, Dan, owning forty-nine percent of the shares in a company can leave you in an extremely vulnerable position."

"Yes, it can, can't it?" he said quietly. "Oh, *hell*, Corinne, why are you doing this?" He tugged at the knot of his tie, pulling it down and unfastening the top button of his shirt. His lean, tanned fingers reached up to knead the taut muscles of his neck.

Her heart gave the infuriating leap that his most casual actions so often evoked, but she dismissed it as a symptom of nerves. "I'm doing what I think is in the best interests of the Dansted Corporation," she said.

He walked over to the window and stared silently out at the parking lot. "You know I can't continue as president of this company unless I have the authority to make my decisions stick," he said. He turned slowly, leaning wearily against the window frame as he looked at her. "So what do you suggest we do now, Corinne? What do you want from me?"

She wanted to cross the room and rest her head against the broad strength of his shoulders. She wanted to touch her fingers to the tightly controlled line of his mouth. She wanted to feel his lips part as they had on Saturday, and to feel his tongue curling around her fingertip. She wanted . . .

Corinne swung away abruptly, drawing in a deep breath. "There's a very easy solution to our problems," she said, pitching her words low, so that at least she sounded calm, despite the roller-coaster churning of her stomach. "It's one that would work well for both of us. If you married me, and agreed to become the father of my child, then the Dansted Corporation would be yours to run precisely as you see fit. You'd not only be president, you would also own all of the shares. Your power would be absolute."

Dan's hands clenched into fists. "Corinne . . . for God's sake! I thought I'd made it clear that I'm not interested in becoming some bizarre kind of walking sperm bank. I thought you agreed—"

"I agree that if you'll give me a child, I'll give you my shares in the Dansted Corporation. A straightforward, even exchange."

"You'll *give* me your shares? You'll give me some-thing I was originally prepared to pay you three million dollars for?"

"The money isn't very important to me, and I'm not giving you the shares. I'm trading them for something I want much more than money."

The silence seemed endless. Watching Dan closely, she saw the precise moment when his rigid self-control finally snapped. He slammed his fist onto the windowsill, then laughed—a brief, harsh sound totally devoid of humor. "You know what, Corinne? You're crazy. But why should I care? Why should I keep playing the noble white knight who's trying to make you see reason? You want me to impregnate you? Lady, you have yourself a deal. I've never taken a crazy woman to bed before, but I'm willing to try anything once. Who knows? Maybe I'm kinkier than I ever suspected. Maybe I'll find out that crazy women turn me on."

Corinne's heart thumped violently for a second or so, and then her whole body seemed to freeze into numbness. "Does that . . . does that mean you agree to my proposal?"

Dan's mouth twisted sardonically. "Sure, why not? If you don't mind telling your child that it was conceived because of some tough bargaining over a Mexican plumb-ing company, then I sure as hell don't see why I should be bothered. Get your purse and your jacket, my dear. I'll drive you back to your motel and get to work on my assignment right away."

Her voice seemed to echo from the end of a long tunnel. "You don't want to risk impregnating me before the wedding," Corinne heard herself say. "I might renege on our bargain."

Of course, that wasn't the real reason for her reluc-tance to go to bed with him before their wedding ceremony, but she wasn't about to reveal the truth at this delicate stage in their negotiations.

She heard his footsteps halt abruptly, halfway to the door. "Corinne," he said slowly, "this is the last time I'm going to ask. Are you quite sure this is what you want?"

"Yes," she said, without looking at him. "Yes, I'm quite sure."

He came back into the room and sat down behind his desk. One glance at his face was sufficient to show that he had his emotions firmly under control again. "Why don't you take a seat," he said formally. "There are some details we need to discuss."

She sat in the chair he indicated. Dan pulled his calendar toward him and flipped through the pages. "I have to go to Mexico next week," he said. "And the weekend after that I'm scheduled to give a speech at the Hardware Manufacturers' convention. How about if we set Saturday, July twenty-second as our wedding day? That should give the lawyers time to get all the paperwork in order."

"That sounds . . ." Her throat wasn't functioning properly, so she swallowed hard and tried again. "That sounds perfectly convenient for me," she said.

"Good." He made a quick notation on his calendar, as if otherwise he might forget his own wedding day, then pushed the diary casually to one side. "I guess the next thing we should discuss is what terms we want to include in our prenuptial agreement."

Corinne was determined to sound as businesslike as he did. "I've already given that some thought, and I believe we only need two basic clauses: one to make sure you don't try to divorce me until I've had my baby, and the other to make sure I don't try to reclaim the Dansted Corporation shares as part of the financial settlement at the time of our divorce."

Dan nodded briefly. "Provided you don't mind some tough language in the premarital contract, Frank shouldn't have any difficulty drawing up a document that effectively denies you any rights to the shares once you've assigned them to me."

"I told you before, I trust Frank and I'll sign anything he says is fair and reasonable."

Corinne was feeling hot, bothered, and thoroughly flustered, but Dan seemed quite detached and remarkably free of embarrassment as he leaned back in his chair, legs stretched out comfortably to one side of the desk.

"Since my services as an impregnator are commanding three million dollars, I think you have a right to know what you're buying. I have every reason to believe I'm medically capable of fathering a child, but I'll check with my doctor and provide you with a certificate of confirmation." He looked at her blandly. "Do you anticipate any problems in becoming a mother?"

Corinne decided she was definitely not cut out for this sort of negotiation. She could feel her face flushing from flaming scarlet to apopleptic purple, but when you got right down to it, there was simply no delicate way to discuss the details of their bargain. "Er . . . no. I don't . . . um . . . anticipate any problems. My gynecologist seems to think I'm aggressively healthy and an ideal candidate for motherhood."

"Then would it be reasonable to include a clause in our contract stipulating that we should stay married for two years, or until your child is born, whichever comes first? Otherwise, if by any remote chance you didn't become pregnant, we might find ourselves tied to each other for life."

"Two years seems more than long enough," Corinne agreed. A new and awful thought occurred to her. Was

Dan expecting her to sit across Frank Goldberg's desk and *explain* these prenuptial contract clauses to him? Stronger spirits than hers would surely have quailed at the prospect. She fanned her burning cheeks with her notepad.

"Do you think it might be a good idea to have two separate prenuptial contracts?" she suggested faintly. "Frank could draw up the one dealing with the shares, and then we could find another lawyer who would take care of the more personal details of our agreement."

Dan reflected for a moment. "Yes," he said finally. "That would probably be a good idea from everybody's point of view. Frank's real expertise is basically limited to company law."

Corinne smothered a sigh of relief. "There is one other thing, Dan, although it's not strictly a legal matter. I think it would look a little strange if I continued living in the motel once people know that we're married. Would you mind very much if I moved into your apartment? I'm only talking about transferring a couple of suitcases, nothing major. And the apartment's big enough that we wouldn't have to see each other very often . . ."

"Except in the bedroom, of course," Dan said dryly. "You're paying me three million dollars, Corinne. Hardly a trifling sum. Naturally, I feel obligated to take my responsibilities seriously. I figure that with a little hard work and dedication to duty, it shouldn't take more than a couple of months to get you pregnant. What do you think?"

Corinne swallowed hard. "I believe three months is considered normal for a healthy married couple." Her voice, she realized despairingly, had once again reverted to a hollow squeak.

"Ah well, I guess a million dollars a month isn't a bad rate of pay."

The words were coolly spoken and laced with typical self-mockery, but some undercurrent in his tone finally penetrated the haze of embarrassment enveloping Corinne. Looking up quickly, she caught a flicker of hot, hard anger in Dan's eyes before his face regained its usual controlled expression. Oddly enough, she was almost glad to discover he wasn't handling their conversation with the total lack of emotion his outward appearance suggested.

Dan rose to his feet. "Unless there's anything else you have an urgent need to discuss, I've got a meeting in Providence at two o'clock and I ought to be leaving. I'll see Frank this evening and start him on the legal paperwork."

"No, I don't think there's anything else we need to discuss," she said, rising from her chair. They faced each other awkwardly in the middle of the room. After an almost imperceptible hesitation, Dan extended his hand. "I hope this deal works out to your satisfaction, Corinne."

"Thank you," she said, shaking his hand quickly. "I'm sure it will."

There was a tap on the door, and then Alma poked her gray head around the opening. "Dan, I thought you'd like a reminder of your appointment in Providence."

"I'm just leaving," he said, casually disengaging his hand from Corinne's clasp. "Oh, by the way, Alma, I'd like you to be the first to know. Corinne has just agreed to marry me. We're very happy about it, aren't we, darling?"

He was out of the office before either Alma or Corinne could recover her voice.

Chapter Eight

ALMA REGAINED HER powers of speech first, and she used
them to outstanding effect. Without batting an eyelash,
she announced that she'd known all along that Corinne
and Dan were madly in love. Then, scarcely pausing for
breath, she also informed Corinne that she was intimately
acquainted with all the best shopping centers in Rhode
Island, Massachussetts, and Connecticut, and she begged
to be taken along when Corinne went searching for her
wedding dress.

Corinne mumbled something about not planning a big
wedding, to which Alma replied, "Nonsense, of course
you are," and rushed from the office, her face wreathed
in smiles.

Within fifteen minutes Alma had personally informed
everybody in the immediate vicinity that Dan Matthews
and Corinne Steddon were getting married. Within an
hour the office grapevine had carried the news to every
employee of the Dansted Corporation. Somebody even
remembered to call the security guards and the weekend
janitor to let them in on the not-so-secret secret.

By five o'clock Corinne had listened to all the congratulations and good wishes she could cope with for
one day. She was more than a little appalled by the furor
the news had aroused. She and Dan had both been a bit

naive, she reflected, lifting her jacket from the tree stand. The Dansted Corporation was still small enough that everybody knew everybody else, and there was no way a marriage between the president and his partner's widow could go unremarked. In view of the real circumstances of their projected marriage, the employees' enthusiasm was disconcerting to say the least.

The phone rang just as she was about to leave her office for the day. She reached for the receiver with a sigh. The prospect of a long soak in a bathtub full of scented bubbles had rarely seemed so appealing.

"Hello. This is Corinne Steddon."

"And this is Martha Matthews. I've just heard the most astonishing news. Is it true?"

Corinne's fingers tightened around the phone, and her whole body suddenly felt stiff and awkward. Those few booming words were sufficient to transport her back seven years to the early days of her marriage to Charlie when Martha Matthews—Dan's mother, and the sister of Charlie's first wife—had flown out to Denver with the declared intention of inspecting Charlie's second bride.

From the moment of her arrival in Denver, Mrs. Matthews had made no secret of the fact that she found Corinne hopelessly unqualified for the honor Charlie had bestowed on her. And Corinne, bristling with insecurity beneath her tough, hard-mouthed exterior, had barely managed to endure that unpleasant forty-eight hours.

It was during Mrs. Matthew's visit, however, that Corinne had truly begun to love Charlie. He had borne his sister-in-law's rudeness with unending courtesy, never failing to offer Corinne all the support and encouragement she needed. Afterwards, when Martha Matthews finally departed, he'd dismissed Corinne's apologies for the disastrous visit with a warm, understanding smile.

"You behaved perfectly," he said.

When she raised a disbelieving eyebrow, he grinned cheerfully. "Well, *almost* perfectly, considering the provocation. Don't worry about a thing, honey. Just try to remember that my sister-in-law is a very unhappy woman."

An angry question from Martha Matthews jolted Corinne back to the present. "Yes, I'm here, Mrs. Matthews," she said quietly into the phone. "I'm sorry I didn't answer you sooner."

"I heard the most extraordinary and disturbing rumor this afternoon. Somebody told me you're planning to marry my son."

Not to mention the fact that I'm planning to make you an almost instant grandmother, Corinne reflected wryly. The thought sent a hot curl of anticipation shooting through her body.

She ignored the anticipation and concentrated on keeping her voice calm and pleasant. "I'm sorry you received the news in such a startling fashion, Mrs. Matthews. I'm sure Dan was planning to tell you in person as soon as he got back from his meeting."

"You mean the information is true? You and Dan . . . you and my son are going to be married?"

There were many cutting responses she could have made, but Corinne decided she could afford to be gracious. "I'll do my very best to make Dan happy, Mrs. Matthews. I very much want to be a good wife to him."

Even though their marriage would be brief, her promise was sincere. She sensed intuitively that Dan's first marriage had left him badly scarred and distrustful of women, and she was determined to show him that women could be honest, straightforward, and completely trustworthy in their dealings.

"Dan is my only son. I can't understand why he didn't call me," Mrs. Matthews said, sounding genuinely bewildered.

"We only decided to get married at lunchtime today," Corinne replied gently. With a surge of relief, she heard the unmistakable sound of Dan's firm footsteps passing her door on the way to his own office. "I believe Dan has just arrived back from Providence, Mrs. Matthews. If you hold on a moment, I know he'll want to speak with you."

When Corinne hurried into the corridor, Dan gave her a quick, intense look that started a slow fire deep in the pit of her stomach. She turned away, struggling for control. "Dan, your mother is on the phone. She heard about . . . she heard we're planning to get married, and she's anxious to speak to you."

His gaze became shuttered. "I'll pick up the call on my extension," he said. "But, Corinne, please wait for me. I'd like to talk to you before you leave."

She sat on the sofa in her office, listening to the thunder of her heartbeat and pretending to read a magazine until he joined her about ten minutes later.

"My mother wants us to have dinner with her on Thursday at her house," he said abruptly. "She's inviting my sisters and their husbands. I'm sorry, Corinne, but there was no way I could get out of it without hurting her feelings."

"I understand," she said, although she was dismayed by this new evidence of how far out of control events seemed to have spiraled. In less than five hours, a private arrangement between her and Dan had somehow become a public happening, involving dozens of other people. She managed a somewhat uncertain smile.

"I guess we forgot about families and friends when

we were making our plans this morning."

"We forgot about a lot of things," he said. He walked over to the embroidered silk wall-hanging and absent-mindedly stroked the tassels knotted at the corner. "I had time to do some thinking during the drive to Providence," he said. "I've decided I want to have joint custody of our child when it's born. Do you still agree to that?"

"Yes," she said softly. "We can work out some sort of joint-custody arrangement."

"Good." Noticing what he was doing with the silken tassels, he pushed his hands into his trouser pockets. He crossed briskly to the coffee table and snapped open his briefcase. "Here's a copy of my schedule for the next two weeks. As you can see, I'm not going to be in town very often. We need to decide which state we're going to be married in, so that we can have the blood tests and arrange for the license."

"It really doesn't matter to me, Dan."

"Take a couple of days to think about it. Connecticut has slightly more flexible grounds for divorce than Rhode Island, if that's a consideration. I'm going to be in New York tomorrow and Thursday morning, but I'll pick you up at your motel at about five on Thursday afternoon. We can finalize the wedding arrangements while we're driving to my mother's place."

"Sounds good to me."

Corinne stood up just as Dan leaned over to shut his briefcase, and for a moment their bodies touched from shoulder to thigh. Heat flared instantly under her skin, before they both jerked back.

"Well, I'd better get going," Dan said quickly. "Frank is waiting for me in his office. We have to get moving right away on all those legal documents."

"Yes, of course." Corinne smiled brightly. "I'll see

you on Thursday, at about five o'clock. I'll wait in the motel lobby, so you won't need to park."

Five minutes after being introduced to Dan's sisters, Corinne realized that she and Dan had just wasted the two hours they had spent planning a quiet wedding in a judge's chambers. Kate and Linda were tall and brown haired like their brother, with fragile, heart-shaped faces and melting brown eyes.

Despite the fragility of their features, they were without doubt the most determined women Corinne had ever encountered. Moreover, they had obviously devoted the past three days to the task of organizing a wedding ceremony that their brother would never forget. In this, Dan's mother was their staunch ally.

Ten minutes of the cocktail hour were devoted to the boring social necessity of performing introductions, offering congratulations, and making polite small talk. Kate and Linda then cut ruthlessly to the matter at hand, which—as far as they were concerned—was the need to organize a wedding for a minimum of fifty guests in only two weeks.

"It would make things much easier, Dan, if you'd only delay the ceremony for a few weeks," Linda suggested. "Corinne, would you mind very much if the date was moved to August?"

Dan put his arm around Corinne's waist and dropped a light kiss on the end of her nose. *"I'd* mind," he said, giving her one of the smiles that always made her feel as if her bones were slowly dissolving. "Corinne and I are getting married on the twenty-second, Linda. We don't plan to wait any longer than that."

Linda's eyes twinkled. "Oh, Lord! True love," she said good-naturedly. "I'd almost forgotten what it's like."

Corinne wondered bleakly what Dan's sisters would say if they knew that their brother's touching eagerness was caused by his desire to get the marriage over with, not his desire to get it started. However, she wasn't allowed any time to brood over her thoughts. Mrs. Matthews and her daughters seemed undaunted by Dan's flat assertion that the wedding date could not be postponed. They merely pressed ahead even more energetically with their plans.

By the time everybody had eaten the first course of iced soup, Corinne and Dan had already agreed that the wedding would be held in the garden and that Mrs. Matthews's minister would perform the ceremony. Long before anybody had finished the main course of smoked turkey, Corinne and Dan had somehow agreed that seventy guests would be a reasonable number to invite. By the time strawberries and cream arrived for dessert, Corinne had almost given up fighting against the tidal wave of Kate and Linda's enthusiasm. She sought Dan's eyes in a half-desperate, half-laughing appeal for sympathy as Kate blithely volunteered the services of her eldest daughter as flower girl. Coward that he was, Dan simply shrugged his shoulders apologetically and helped himself to more strawberries.

By the time Mrs. Matthews brought in the coffee, Corinne had somehow agreed that not only would Jennifer make a perfect flower girl but Linda's son, William, would be positively angelic as ring bearer.

"Then it's all settled," Mrs. Matthews said majestically as Dan and Corinne made their somewhat flustered farewells. "If you'll let me have your guest list, Corinne, I'll see to invitations and everything else."

"Mother, really, Corinne and I only want—"

"All you have to do, Dan, is take care of the honeymoon arrangements; and all you have to do, Corinne, is take care of your dress."

"We'll organize all the flowers," Linda called out. "One of my old school friends has a flower shop right here in town."

"How convenient," Corinne said hollowly.

Five minutes later Dan turned the Mazda out of his mother's driveway and let out an explosive sigh. "My God, Corinne, I'm so sorry!"

She looked at him, and suddenly her shoulders started to shake with laughter. "Dan, I hate to say this, but your sisters are the most *terrifying* women! Good Lord, if the Pentagon hired them, no weapons system would ever run over budget again."

He grinned. "They're not usually so pushy. Weddings seem to bring out the dragon in both of them." He paused for a minute. "Will the fuss bother you too much? I can put a stop to it if you really don't want a big wedding."

"No, that's okay. It seems to be giving them so much pleasure. I just feel a bit fraudulent, knowing how everything's going to end."

"The outcome will be the same wherever we marry," he said. "So they may as well have the fun of organizing the ceremony they want."

"I guess."

"Mrs. Diaz accepted our offer for her husband's company," he said. "So I'm leaving for Mexico tomorrow night. I won't be back until next Wednesday."

"I hope everything goes well," she said steadily. Aware of a tiny, painful ache somewhere deep inside her she wondered for a crazy moment if it could be caused by the prospect of spending so many days away from him. But the idea was ridiculous, and she spoke quickly, before it could take root in her mind.

"I probably won't be here when you get back, Dan.

I'll have to fly to Denver next week to settle a few details with Charlie's lawyers. I also have to make arrangements to store the furniture, which I expect will take a while."

"Then we won't be seeing each other until a couple of days before the wedding." Stopping at a traffic light, he turned to look at her. "Take care of yourself, Corinne, and call me in Tampico if you run into any unexpected problems."

Her unexpected problem at this precise moment seemed to be an acute attack of breathlessness. "Thanks for the offer," she said lightly. "But unless Kate decides to hire the Mormon Tabernacle Choir, I think I should be able to handle things."

He laughed wryly. "Bite your tongue," he said. "Be careful what you joke about, or you'll give Kate and Linda ideas."

Debbie Jones and Alma Grady were obviously closet soulmates to Dan's mother and sisters. On Monday morning they presented themselves in Corinne's office wearing sturdy walking sandals, cool cotton dresses, and determined smiles.

"Leslie is covering the switchboard for me," Debbie informed Corinne. "And Alma has taken the day off, too, so we're all set to go shopping. We thought you might need some help since you haven't lived here long enough to know the best places to find a wedding dress."

"But I don't really—"

"We decided that Boston would probably have something suitable," Alma cut in with the ruthless courtesy that made her such an invaluable secretary. "It's quite a long drive, Corinne, so we'd better leave right away."

Alma and Debbie enlivened the trip to Boston with their obvious excitement. They were so enthusiastic that Corinne actually began to share some of their high spirits.

When she walked into the department store they had selected, she felt a spurt of real excitement which she quickly forced back under control. Keeping a firm hold on her common sense, she refused even to look in the special bridal salon, though she did agree to check out the designer gowns and evening wear.

She was delighted when she found a white linen suit that fitted her perfectly. Its cut was elegant, and both the skirt and jacket were lined with pure silk. All in all, she felt that its classic style flattered the tall, slender lines of her body. Emerging from the changing room, she twirled around in front of Alma and Debbie.

"Well, what do you think?"

There was a lengthy pause, and then Alma said flatly. "It's very smart."

"Oh, Corinne, you can't buy that," Debbie murmured simultaneously.

"But what's wrong with it?" Corinne asked, staring at herself in the triple mirror. The suit was crisp, neat, and expensive-looking in a discreet way, and she couldn't imagine why Alma and Debbie seemed so disappointed. "It doesn't even need any alterations," she pointed out.

"And with a navy blue blouse, you could wear it to the office," Alma remarked neutrally.

"Oh," Corinne said. It *was* a bit depressing to think of buying a wedding outfit that could perform double duty as a business suit; but since her whole marriage to Dan was nothing more than a business arrangement, maybe that wasn't such a bad idea. She turned once more to face Debbie and Alma. "It's a very practical choice," she said defensively.

"Couldn't we just *look* in the bridal salon?" Debbie asked wistfully.

"They have an excellent range of styles there, miss,"

the sales assistant interjected tactfully. "Suitable for all different types of weddings."

That was all the encouragement Alma and Debbie needed. Ignoring Corinne's protests, they swept her over to the bridal salon.

"Now this is more like it," Alma announced, indicating an ethereal confection of ruffled white lace. "How do you like it, Corinne?"

"And what about that one!" Debbie breathed, pointing to a heavy satin gown with a seven-foot-long train. "What do you think?"

"I think they're both hopelessly unsuitable," Corinne said dryly.

Debbie and Alma stared at her reprovingly, and she retreated to a chair in the quietest corner of the room, leaving the pair to indulge in an enthusiastic conference with the saleswoman. Her mind was already made up: she would buy the white suit. Alma and Debbie meant well, but she and Dan knew the truth about their relationship and the businesslike linen outfit was ideally suited to this marriage they were planning. It would be embarrassing for both of them if she floated down the aisle in a cloud of white lace. Although, come to think of it, she probably had more right to wear a virginal white gown than most brides nowadays. She wondered, not for the first time, what Dan would say when he discovered she was a virgin. Somehow she had a distinct suspicion he would not be very pleased.

She glanced up at Debbie and Alma, who were now lost in contemplation of a wedding gown designed to look like a Victorian crinoline. Corinne barely managed to smother her laugh. The dress might, just possibly, have been suitable for a wedding held in a cathedral with a minimum of three hundred guests. For a simple garden ceremony, it was ludicrously out of place.

As she let her gaze wander over the glass-covered display cases, she caught sight of an exceptionally pretty gown displayed in the far corner. Of palest cream voile, it had a low neck and short sleeves and was ideally suited to a hot summer wedding. The bodice was plain, but the skirt flowed out in soft folds, ending in a single ruffle that just barely revealed a frill of lace beneath.

Trancelike, Corinne felt herself standing up and walking over to the saleswoman. "I'd like to try on that voile dress over there. I wear a size ten. Do you have it in stock by any chance?"

"Yes, miss, we certainly do." In record time, the sales assistant had taken Corinne into the large bridal dressing room and helped her into the dress. The assistant adjusted the folds of the skirt, then sighed with satisfaction.

"Take a look in the mirror, miss. I think you've found the perfect dress, if you don't mind me saying so."

Corinne stared at the starry-eyed, pink-cheeked girl in the mirror. Don't let yourself be carried away by the fantasy, she warned herself, but her cheeks remained flushed, and her eyes still shone with the reflection of her most secret dreams. Hesitantly, she opened the curtains of the dressing room and turned slowly to face Alma and Debbie.

They were as silent as they had been before, and Corinne laughed nervously to hide her disappointment. "Well, ladies, it's this or the white linen suit. Take your pick."

Debbie finally broke her silence. "It's stunning, Corinne. You look truly beautiful. With your blonde hair, that color looks better on you than stark white."

"And I've already seen the perfect hat," Alma put in. She darted away and came back triumphantly. "See," she said, holding up a wide-brimmed straw hat, bedecked with satin ribbons and peach-colored rosebuds.

"Put it on, miss," the shop assistant encouraged. "You're really in luck. The straw is exactly the same shade as the dress, and that almost never happens. Of course, you'll have to wear your hair loose if you want the hat to fit properly."

Debbie and Alma couldn't stop congratulating themselves when the assistant finally finished adjusting the hat and sent Corinne back out for their inspection. "Dan is going to be absolutely devastated when he sees how beautiful you look," Debbie said. She gave a deep, romantic sigh.

Corinne forced herself to smile casually. "I think Dan and I are both a bit past the stage of being devastated," she said, determined not to allow herself to venture any deeper into the fantasy that Alma and Debbie were so eager to construct. She glanced down at her watch, forcing herself to behave practically. "It's two o'clock already. How about a quick lunch before we go back to the office?"

Corinne didn't escape from the mounting pressures of the wedding preparations until she took off from Logan Airport for Denver two hours before Dan was scheduled to return from Mexico. With all the problems involved in putting Charlie's house on the market and storing her furniture, she'd been easily able to justify remaining in Colorado until Thursday of the following week.

When her plane landed again at Logan, Corinne found Dan waiting for her at the arrivals gate. She hadn't expected him to meet her, and for one wild moment she allowed herself to hope he'd come because he cared and was eager to see her again. Her heart jumped, and all the breath seemed to rush out of her lungs. During the brief time they had been apart, she had somehow managed to forget how impossibly virile he always looked in his conservative dark suits. He smiled as soon as she appeared, but instead of rushing forward to greet her, he remained standing outside the gate area until she reached him. He held out his hand. Corinne shook it politely and hoped to God that she looked a bit less flustered than she felt.

"Alma told me what plane you were taking," he said. "The lawyer who drew up our prenuptial contract works right here in Boston, and since time's getting short, I've arranged for us to meet him this afternoon at his office. That way we can get everything signed before we leave for my mother's house tomorrow afternoon."

She kept her gaze fixed straight ahead of her. "What a good idea," she said, walking quickly to keep up with his long, swift strides. "Very practical of you."

Had she really thought, even for a moment, that Dan had come to the airport because he couldn't wait to see her again? Hadn't she gotten it through her thick skull yet that it would be disastrous for both of them if they allowed their emotions to become entangled in their businesslike relationship?

They collected her luggage and went out to the parking lot. Dan talked about the details of the new Mexican joint venture as he drove expertly through the congested Boston streets to the center of town.

The lawyer was middle-aged, dignified and, as far as Corinne could judge, totally unmoved by the bizarre contents of the documents he had drawn up. The contracts contained precisely the provisions she and Dan had agreed to, spelled out in meticulous and embarrassing detail. Within half an hour all the copies had been signed, and then Dan was once more courteously escorting Corinne out to his car.

"I'm sorry to drag you around to so many different places," he said, "but Frank is waiting for us at the office with the other contract. That one lists all the conditions Charlie imposed for the transfer of the shares, so it will take you a bit longer to go through it, I'm afraid."

"We have all evening," she said, not looking at him. "Unless you have other plans?"

"No. I don't have any plans until I drive you to my mother's house tomorrow." He glanced to his left, then edged the car into the fast lane. "She tells me your wedding dress was delivered last week and that it's very beautiful. That's high praise, coming from my mother."

Corinne's throat tightened. "I'm pleased she approves," she said. "I hope you'll like it, too." She could have bitten her tongue off as soon as she'd spoken.

"I'm sure I will," Dan said neutrally. "You have excellent taste." He glanced at the clock in the dashboard. "We've made good time, so we should be in Frank's office a few minutes early."

It was only five-thirty when they arrived at Dansted Corporation headquarters, but the building seemed deserted. They headed straight for Frank's office.

"Glad to have you back again," the lawyer said, shaking Corinne's hand and patting her heartily on the shoulder. "Dan here has been like an old bear with a sore paw since he returned from Mexico. We'll all be glad when you take him away on his honeymoon and make him happy again."

"Frank . . ." Dan said warningly.

The lawyer seemed not a whit abashed. He winked at Corinne, then seated himself cheerfully behind his desk. "Well, let's get right to work, my dear. Here are the contracts Dan asked me to draw up. I'm sure you'd like a few minutes to read them through. I should point out that even if you sign these contracts tonight, they won't go into effect until you and Dan are actually married. And don't hesitate to ask if you have any questions—anything at all."

"Thank you," Corinne said, taking the papers. She settled down into the chair and began to read. After a couple of minutes she felt the color drain from her cheeks, and she looked up at Dan.

"You've paid me for my shares," she said. "You've paid me a million dollars."

"Yes." His voice was clipped. "I preferred to keep strictly to the terms of Charlie's will. As you can see, the million dollars goes into a trust fund and never becomes part of our joint marital property. That way, whatever happens to us in the future, the money will always be yours."

Corinne held herself perfectly still, although inside she was shaking. He had put the money into a trust fund so that when they got divorced he would have no possible means of reclaiming it. "That wasn't necessary, Dan," she said softly. "You know what we agreed."

Frank, naturally, misunderstood their exchange. "Dan is behaving very properly, Corinne. Right now, you're both madly in love, and I'm sure you're anxious to make him a gift of your shares. But property and love are two different things, and a wise person always keeps the two issues separate. Dan is a gentleman, my dear, and he's merely behaving exactly as his uncle would have wished him to behave."

"Cut out the eulogies, Frank. I'm not dead yet."

The lawyer smiled affectionately at Dan, then turned his attention back to Corinne. "If you have any other questions, I'll be happy to answer them. If not, I need your signature in the three places I've marked. Dan must sign, too."

After the contracts were duly signed and notarized, Frank began fiddling with his tie. Corinne wondered why he suddenly seemed so nervous. "I'd like to invite you to join me for dinner," he said. "My wife particularly asked me to bring you both—in fact, she told me I wasn't to take no for an answer."

Dan and Corinne exchanged glances. "It's very kind of you," Dan said, "but with Corinne just arriving from Denver—"

"I absolutely insist," Frank said hurriedly. "The truth is, my wife's organized a little dinner party, and she won't speak to me for a week if I don't bring you home with me."

"Well, we certainly don't want to be responsible for Ellie not speaking to you," Dan said easily, draping an arm around Corinne's shoulder. "Do you think you can keep going for another couple of hours, honey?"

Her shoulder burned where his arm touched her, and she carefully moved away. "I'm sure I can," she said brightly.

"Good, good." Frank beamed jovially. "I'll just give Ellie a call and let her know we're on our way."

Frank's home was a pleasant suburban ranch, built on two acres of wooded land. Despite the rural setting, the road leading up to his house was jammed with parked cars.

"I wonder why there are so many cars." Corinne said.

"I'm beginning to think I know *exactly* why," Dan replied grimly. "Didn't you notice that there wasn't a soul at the office other than Frank?" He got out of the car and folded his arms with ominous intent, waiting for the lawyer to approach.

"Hey, former friend, would you mind telling me how

many people your wife has invited to her 'small' dinner party?"

"Not that many," Frank said, smiling. "Not that many at all." His nervousness had disappeared now that his mission was almost accomplished. "Come on inside and see for yourself."

When he opened the door, the strains of Mendelssohn's Wedding March immediately blasted forth, almost drowned out by the applause of approximately one hundred Dansted Corporation employees and their spouses, crushed into the house and spilling out to the backyard.

The look Dan gave Corinne was almost comic in its embarrassment. "I'm sorry," he muttered. "Truly sorry. That's all I seem to keep saying to you these days."

"It doesn't matter," she said, and found to her surprise that the words were true. She was touched by the evidence of so much affection and interest on the part of their colleagues.

She was less happy when Ellie Goldberg, Alma, and two catering assistants carried out the huge ice-cream cake that had been ordered for dessert. "Cut the cake," Ellie ordered with a friendly smile. She handed Corinne a sharp silver knife that had been dipped in hot water. "You help her, Dan. It'll be practice."

Corinne reluctantly picked up the knife as Dan stood behind her, his body touching hers along the entire length of her spine. He had discarded his jacket and tie and unbuttoned his shirt almost to the waist, and she could feel the heat of his body through her thin blouse, prickling against her skin.

Dan seemed indifferent to their closeness. "Ready?" he asked.

She nodded, and his arms came around her, his fingers closing over her knuckles, warm and strong as he helped push the blade through the frozen cake. Ellie held out a plate to receive the first slice, and Corinne suddenly became aware of the expectant hush that had fallen over the crowd of guests.

"It's no good, Corinne. I can't think of a single way to get out of this," Dan murmured into her ear.

Startled, she put down the knife, looking up at him as he slowly twisted her around in his arms. It was only when they were face-to-face that she realized he was going to kiss her.

No big deal, she told herself firmly. With a hundred people looking on, this kiss wasn't going to set anybody's pulse racing. Dan's head bent with tantalizing slowness toward her mouth, and her eyes drifted closed. In just a minute she would open them, she told herself. But not quite yet.

His fingers spread wide on her back, and a hand trailed upward to twine in her hair. His mouth covered hers, moving against her lips with restless, compelling urgency. "Open your mouth for me," he whispered.

She responded mindlessly to his command, and his tongue pressed fiercely between her parted lips. Her heart immediately began to pound in double time, and her legs became traitors that refused to continue supporting her.

Audience or not, this was getting to be a pretty big deal, Corinne realized belatedly. Blood was pounding in her ears, and her breasts were thrusting against Dan's chest. She had no difficulty detecting that he was every bit as aroused as she was. This has got to stop right now, she told herself, right this second. His fingers gently stroked her spine, leaving a trail of liquid fire. Maybe another few moments wouldn't matter, she thought. In just a minute she would move away.

Dan's hands tightened in a sudden, convulsive grip

around her arms and, dazedly, she felt him tear his mouth away.

She blinked, finding it difficult to focus, and realized that the guests were all either applauding or calling out a variety of distinctly earthy comments.

Ellie laughed and handed Corinne a piece of ice-cream cake. "Here," she said. "you and Dan had better eat some of this to cool yourselves off. That was some kiss!"

Dan put the dessert plate back on the table as soon as Ellie left to speak with one of her guests. He cradled Corinne in his arms and bent down, pretending to nuzzle her neck. "Don't move too far away," he said softly, "or I'm going to embarrass both of us."

Heat blazed in her cheeks. This was ridiculous. She'd handled this sort of thing a whole lot better when she was seventeen.

"Did you manage to get everything settled while you were in Denver?" he asked, still holding her loosely.

"Yes. I put the house on the market, much to the delight of the local realty company. They seem to think they'll get a good price for it."

"You don't plan to go back to Colorado when your baby's born?"

"Probably, but that's a long way in the future."

"Maybe not that far," Dan said. "We get married the day after tomorrow."

Something coiled tight and hard in the pit of Corinne's stomach. "Yes," she said. "I remember."

Chapter Nine

DAN DROVE THE Mazda out of his mother's driveway to a hail of rice and the rattling accompaniment of a dozen tin cans. "Can you stand the noise for five minutes?" he asked Corinne. "There's a shopping plaza right before we turn onto the highway, and I should be able to buy a pair of wire clippers there. I'm afraid I know my brothers-in-law only too well—we won't be able to remove those cans with anything short of heavy-duty cutters."

"Yes, of course I can wait." Corinne turned toward Dan, then hurriedly looked away again. She cleared her throat. "By the way, are we going back to your apartment?"

"Only to pack. I thought we might find the explanations awkward if we stayed here and kept bumping into old friends when we're supposed to be on our honeymoon. A business acquaintance of mine has a cottage in Cape Cod, and he's loaned it to us until the end of next week."

"That was kind of him," Corinne said mechanically.

Their awkward conversation lapsed into total silence until Dan parked outside a hardware store in the shopping center. "Why don't you wait in the car?" he suggested. "I'll only be a couple of minutes."

Corinne nodded her agreement, then watched as he strode quickly into the store. A woman exited through the glass doors carrying a straw broom. She was followed by a middle-aged man wearing baggy shorts, an oil-stained T-shirt, and a pair of battered sneakers. Corinne touched the low neckline of her turquoise silk dress and thought how odd it was that while she and Dan had been getting married, other people had been busy mowing their lawns, fixing their cars, and doing all the usual Saturday afternoon chores.

Dan returned with the wire cutters and, after a brief struggle under the rear bumper, triumphantly removed the cans and dumped them into the nearest trash barrel. "If we can find a car wash, we'll be home free," he said, easing back into the driver's seat.

Corinne regarded the lipstick-scrawled messages that covered the hood and trunk. "A car wash would be nice," she agreed, then cursed herself for the total inanity of her response. She stroked the engraved gold band Dan had put on her finger that morning and reflected sadly that she hadn't managed to produce any halfway intelligent conversation since she'd walked down the aisle and seen Dan waiting for her, immaculate in a white summer tuxedo.

The rest of their drive passed with no greater ease than the first few miles, their conversation wavering between the excruciatingly stilted and the totally nonexistent. A little too late, Corinne was beginning to realize that several crucial subjects had been ignored in their premarital negotiations.

The basic problem, she admitted ruefully, was that she was experiencing an acute attack of wedding-night jitters. It was darned inconvenient to be a twenty-six-year-old widow with the sexual experience of a teenaged virgin. And a very naïve teenager, at that. Her parents' marriage had taught her to associate sex with violence, and that initial impression had only been confirmed when she'd started working in the bar. By the time Charlie'd walked in a few months before her nineteenth birthday, she had probably witnessed more forms of sexual deviance than anybody outside of the Vice Squad.

But precisely because of all she had seen, Corinne's personal experience was extremely limited. When she'd quit school to take care of her mother, her actual first-hand knowledge of sex had amounted to no more than a couple of wet and awkward kisses. After her mother's death, the teenage leader of the local motorcycle gang had forced her into several grim wrestling matches before she wised up and took care never to find herself alone with him. Despite her desire to defy her father, she'd had just enough self-respect to halt her defiance short of having sex with a young hood who was out strictly for his own gratification.

There had been dozens of opportunities for sexual experimentation once she started working at the bar, but she had acquired some street-smarts by that time and knew instinctively that her job would be a lot easier if she acquired a reputation for being unavailable. Her boss had tried halfheartedly to seduce her, and when he failed, Corinne had successfully steered clear of men — until she met Charlie.

The problem was, she knew she had given Dan a very different impression. Naturally enough, he assumed that she'd led a normal married life with Charlie, and she had never corrected that mistaken assumption. She had also told him Charlie wasn't the first man she'd taken home to her apartment. Her words had been true enough, but their implication had been entirely false. The only men she'd taken home had been beaten up in fights outside the bar, and they'd expressed their gratitude strictly in terms of friendship.

"It's only about another ten miles," Dan said, interrupting a long period of silence. "Would you look out for a sign saying Bass River; that's where we turn off."

Fifteen minutes later they drew up outside a pleasant, whitewashed cottage built in typical Cape Cod style. "Well, that was painless," Dan said with an exaggerated sigh of relief. "I think our marriage just passed its first test. Fighting over directions ranks right up there with squeezing the wrong end of the toothpaste as grounds for divorce."

Corinne laughed. "Does it? Maybe you'd better tell me the worst. Do you squeeze your toothpaste from the end, the top, or the middle?"

He regarded her solemnly. "I use one of those new pumps."

"So do I."

Dan grinned. "Then ours is clearly a match made in heaven. Hold on a minute, and I'll get your bags out of the trunk."

The cottage was small, but charming. The ground floor consisted of a utility room, a large kitchen/dining room, and a living room with a stone fireplace. Upstairs, two low-ceilinged and beamed bedrooms were separated by a luxurious, modern bathroom. The views from almost every window were spectacular—particularly to Corinne, who had been twenty years old before she got her first look at the ocean.

She opened the living-room windows and leaned out to smell the salt-laden air. "Mmm . . . It's a pity we've arrived so late. It would be great to go swimming."

"The water will be cold at this time of night, and we

· have all day tomorrow. The weather forecast calls for lots of sunshine."

"That's true." *But first we have to get through tonight.* She drew her head in from the window, hoping her smile didn't look as artificial as it felt. "I don't know about you, but I'm starving. Your sisters ordered all that wonderful food for the reception, yet somehow I never managed to eat any of it."

"There's a local woman who takes care of this cottage. I called yesterday and asked her to stock the fridge. Let's see what she's done for us."

She had obviously done a great deal. They worked companionably together, preparing toasted ham-and-cheese sandwiches and a fresh fruit salad. Dan discovered a bottle of champagne, together with a note of good wishes from his friend, Brent, the owner of the cottage, and Corinne recklessly agreed to share it with him.

They ate at the table by the kitchen window, watching the ocean grow dark as the sun sank slowly in the west. The trees glowed golden against the horizon, then turned into black shadows silhouetted against the night sky. The tranquillity of the scene ought to have been soothing, but somehow the peacefulness of their surroundings only seemed to emphasize her growing tension.

"Let's take the rest of the champagne into the living room," Dan suggested when they'd stacked their plates in the dishwasher.

"All right," she agreed, although she'd already had far more than the one glass of alcohol she normally allowed herself.

Dan put the champagne bottle on a low cocktail table in front of the fireplace and settled into a corner of the sofa. Corinne very gingerly seated herself at the opposite end.

"Pity it's too warm for a fire," he said, stretching out his legs. "That huge fireplace almost makes me wish it was raining outside."

"Yes." Corinne pressed her knees tightly together and tugged the hem of her skirt down. "A fire always makes a room look cozy."

"Brent told me he bought this cottage five years ago and had to rebuild it almost from the foundations up."

"But he's lucky to have found beachfront property in such a prime location. That isn't always easy to do."

"True." Dan stirred his champagne with his forefinger, absently watching the bubbles pop on the surface. He'd long since discarded his jacket and tie. Now he unfastened the top two buttons of his shirt and stretched lazily. "The wedding reception went off quite well, don't you think? All the guests seemed to have a good time."

She took one quick look at the tanned column of his throat, then concentrated hard on staring at her toes. "Yes, your mother and sisters did a fantastic job, and Jennifer made a very pretty flower girl."

"Young William didn't even drop the rings."

"No, he was very good. Linda says they managed to get several cute pictures of him before he wiped chocolate ice cream all over his white pants."

Silence settled over the room with deadly weight, and Corinne took a desperate swig of her champagne. She reflected that for somebody who never drank, she seemed to have a regrettably hard head. So far, the repeated doses of champagne hadn't made her situation seem even marginally less awkward. How ironic that the first time in her life she'd even contemplated getting drunk, her plan wasn't succeeding.

"Dan—"

"Corinne—"

They had spoken simultaneously, and the look Dan

gave her was tinged with wry understanding. "You go first," he said. "Personally, I'm fresh out of things to talk about."

Now was her chance, she thought. If she wasn't careful, they were going to end up in the bedroom before she told him she'd never made love before. She sought frantically for some appropriately casual words, but nothing came to mind. *By the way, Dan, although I was married for seven years, I'm still a virgin,* just didn't seem like a statement to be dropped nonchalantly into the conversational pool.

She walked over to the window, pressing her burning cheeks against the wind-cooled panes. She took another gulp of champagne, more because her throat was dry than because she still harbored any hope of dulling her senses. Every nerve in her body seemed to be tinglingly alive.

"Dan ... about tonight ... when we go to bed ..."

"Yes?"

"You don't have to make love to me tonight," she said. The words came out in a rush, and they weren't at all what she'd intended to say. Why couldn't she tell him the truth? she wondered despairingly. Was it because she suspected that he wouldn't have married her if he'd known she was a virgin?

Hearing the clink of glass on glass, she realized Dan was pouring himself more champagne. "I want to make love to you tonight," he said.

She went still, all breath suspended in her body. "You do?"

"I want to get our first time together over and done with," he said harshly. "Dammit, Corinne, I haven't been so uptight about taking a woman to bed since I was seventeen."

Her breath returned in a swift, painful rush, leaving

a sharp ache somewhere in the region of her ribs. She had no desire to ask herself why she found his words so hurtful. "Why should taking me to bed be more difficult than taking any other woman?" she asked tonelessly.

His mouth twisted into a self-mocking smile. "One million dollars is a hell of a stud fee, my dear, and I'm not sure I can live up to my purchase price. There are only so many ways a male and female can have sex together, and at this moment, I'm finding it tough to think of any way that's so exciting it's worth a million dollars."

She tossed off the last of her champagne in one swift, angry swallow. "You're forgetting something," she said tersely. "You were hired as a prospective father, not as a lover."

"I'm under the impression that it's difficult to become a father without being a lover first."

With infinite care, Corinne set her empty champagne glass on the windowsill. She was no longer able to pretend, even to herself, that she was coping with the situation. She spoke into the comforting blankness of the night-darkened window. "Don't worry, Dan, I'm not planning to rate your performance." She bit her lip, disguising its disastrous tendency to wobble. "I think I'll take a shower," she said, and hurried from the room without giving him a chance to reply.

After fifteen minutes in the shower, Corinne reluctantly conceded that there was a limit to the length of time a person could stand under running water without turning into a prune. She wrapped her wrinkled body in a big bath towel, then opened the door a crack. She poked her nose and one eye around the edge of the door. The bedroom, thank God, was still empty. Sighing with relief, she padded across the carpeted floor and snapped open her suitcase. After rummaging among the neat piles of clothing, she finally found her nightgown and robe tucked away at the bottom. She tossed the slinky satin fabric onto the four-poster bed and stared at it despairingly. What in the world had possessed her to purchase two such outrageous garments? And having committed the insanity of buying them, why in the world had she put them in her suitcase? Did she secretly fantasize that Dan would take one look at her and proclaim she was the most beautiful, desirable woman he had ever seen?

She snorted angrily, snatched the offending garments off the bed, and stomped into the bathroom. She hung up the towel, cleaned her teeth, combed her hair, and reluctantly slipped on the white nightgown. It slithered down her body with a sensuous rustle, curling demurely around her ankles and leaving her almost naked from the waist up. Hastily she put on the matching robe, tying it as tightly as possible around her narrow waist. She glanced into the steamy mirror. The satin still hugged her more smoothly around the hips than she would have liked, but at least her breasts were now decently covered.

She had only just returned to the bedroom when there was a light tap on the door. "Come in," she said, hurriedly turning her back.

"It's almost midnight," Dan said. "I thought I'd take a quick shower."

"Yes, why not?" she replied, still staring at the wall. She remained where she was until she heard the shower water running, then walked across to the bed and plumped herself nervously on the edge of the mattress. She pleated the satin ribbons of her robe into a tight ball, then smoothed them out again with ice-cold fingers. Hearing the sound of the bathroom door opening, she looked up, almost paralyzed with nervous tension.

Dan was wearing judo-style black satin pajamas, loosely belted at the waist. She glanced at him once, hurriedly, then looked away and began playing with the ribbons of her robe again. Even when she realized the mindlessness of what she was doing, she didn't seem able to stop.

She heard him flip off the bathroom light, then walk quietly to the bed. He put out his hands and gripped her arms, gently pulling her to her feet. Instinctively she averted his gaze, and he crooked his finger under her chin, turning her around and stroking his thumbs rhythmically across her cheekbones.

"Corinne," he said softly, "maybe this will be easier for both of us if I admit that I've been wanting to make love to you for a very long time."

"You don't have to lie for my sake," she said quickly. "Soothing my ego wasn't part of our deal."

His mouth quirked with a definite hint of impatience. "Forget about our deal for a few minutes, can't you, Corinne? I wasn't lying. Surely you know me well enough by now to realize that I would never have agreed to your proposition unless I'd already decided you were one of the few women I would ever want to become the mother of my child."

She drew in a shaky breath. "I hoped you'd feel that way. I'm going to be a good mother, Dan, I promise."

"I know you are. Our child will be very lucky. You're not only one of the most beautiful women I've ever met; you're intelligent and kindhearted into the bargain." Laughter gleamed momentarily in his eyes. "You're also crazy, of course, but I've decided that no one's perfect."

If he was lying, his lies sounded wonderfully sweet, and she wanted so much to believe him. "Dan," she whispered. "Hold me. I've never done this before, and I'm scared."

"So am I," he replied with a rueful smile, taking her hand and holding it against his chest. "Can you feel how my heart's pounding?" He carried her hand to his lips and pressed a swift kiss into her palm. "I really want this to be good for you, Corinne. I want it to be good for both of us."

He obviously hadn't taken her remark as literally as he should have, Corinne thought nervously, and she couldn't find the courage to make her meaning any more plain. She was too uptight at this point to go into any lengthy explanations anyway. Besides, it was possible she was making too much out of something Dan would consider unimportant. Maybe he wouldn't even realize she was a virgin. Nowadays, many women were so active that she knew there was often no physical evidence the first time they made love. Perhaps she would be one of those women.

Dan traced the outline of her mouth with his thumbs. "What are you thinking about? Your face is very solemn."

She drew in a deep breath. "Nothing important."

He looked at her in silence for a long moment and then, still without speaking, bent forward and untied the sash of her robe. Slowly, deliberately, he slipped his hands inside the lapels and pulled her toward him.

She leaned against him, her eyes closed, and he slowly lowered his head. He moved his lips with tender expertise over her quivering mouth. She parted her lips, and his taste filled her, seeping into every pore of her body. She trembled as small waves of pleasure washed over her, each more powerful than the one before. Her body began to feel slumbrous and heavy, and she stirred restlessly in Dan's arms, seeking relief from the strange, pleasurable tension his kiss was creating.

A cool sea breeze drifted through the open window and struck the bare skin of her shoulders, but she didn't feel the chill. She didn't even realize that Dan's expert hands had already stroked away her robe and tossed it carelessly onto a chair. She only knew that her breasts felt taut and heavy, aching with the need for his touch. She only knew that she wanted to lie down on the bed and hold his head captive between her hands, urging him to suckle.

He was too experienced a lover not to sense her mounting desire. Deepening the kiss, he thrust his tongue into her mouth with unmistakable masculine command, and a hot, voluptuous weakness seized her as he tightened his arms around her waist. His hands lost their gentleness and moved demandingly against her hips, holding her so close that she couldn't avoid feeling the heated power of his arousal. She gasped against his mouth, not frightened, but overwhelmed by the intensity of the new sensations he was creating. Running her fingers down his back, she felt the slickness of sweat beginning to gather at the base of his spine. A fierce, answering heat built rapidly inside her, and her hips began to undulate instinctively against him.

"Oh God, Corinne, no more," he said harshly. "Don't move."

Dazed, not understanding what she had done, she went absolutely still. He carefully eased a few inches away from her.

"I know you're not ready yet, sweetheart," he murmured. "And I'm much more ready than I want to be."

He pushed the thin straps of her nightgown over her shoulders. Vaguely, she was aware of the garment falling in a heap at her feet. She swayed toward him, and he kissed the hollows of her throat as he put his arm beneath her knees and picked her up, carrying her the few steps to the bed. He pulled back the covers, then impatiently shrugged out of his pajamas and lay down beside her. She stretched langorously against the cotton sheets, aware of a delightful sensation of power when she saw his gaze avidly follow her provocative movements.

His eyes glowed with a dark silver fire. "You're even more beautiful than I imagined," he said, and the hoarseness of his voice convinced her that—at least for this brief moment—he found her truly beautiful. He stroked a strand of her pale gold hair. "I've fantasized about seeing your hair spread out on the pillow like this..."

"There's no need for fantasies now," she whispered, turning into his arms.

He held her close for a moment, then took one of her nipples deep into his mouth. Corinne heard herself moan, an anguished cry of pleasure that she could neither stop nor control. As his hands traveled slowly down the length of her body, the fleeting, intimate caresses left her aching, trembling, and begging for more. He traced the slender curve of her waist, then circled gradually, inexorably downward. When he parted her thighs, Corinne gasped, arching wildly against his hand. The sensations he provoked were so intense they were almost painful.

"Dan, please... I don't want... I can't..."

He stopped her breathless words with a kiss. "Yes, you can," he said in a rough whisper. "Darling, let go. Come for me."

His endearment brought her shuddering to the brink of ecstasy. Her fists clenched against his chest as she submitted to the final, burning intimacies of his touch, and she wimpered softly as her body writhed in blissful, trembling fulfillment.

She felt herself go limp with release, but Dan didn't free her mouth from their kiss. He poised himself over her body and thrust into her with a single powerful movement. She cried out, unable to prevent the harsh sound that tore from her throat. Dan tensed, and she felt shock and hesitation shudder through his entire body.

But it was too late for hesitation, too late for second thoughts. His control had reached its limits, and his kiss exploded against her mouth as he surged inside her. He took her swiftly, almost roughly, his body shuddering in her embrace as he reached his climax. Then he rolled off her and sat up straight on the edge of the bed. After a few tense seconds, he spoke into the unnatural quiet of the bedroom.

"Dammit to hell, Corinne. Why didn't you tell me?"

Chapter Ten

DAN SMOTHERED AN acute attack of guilty conscience. There was no way he could have guessed Corinne was a virgin, he assured himself. Dammit, she had been married for seven years. Why in the world would anybody expect her to be a virgin! And nothing in her behavior had prepared him for the truth. In fact, once they'd started making love, her responses had been so passionate that his only concern had been how to extend their foreplay long enough to ensure her pleasure.

Dan was shaken by a fresh spurt of anger as he remembered how roughly he had thrust into her. How could she have been so foolish as to leave him in ignorance of her virginity? Didn't she realize he might have hurt her—and hurt her badly?

Maybe he *had* hurt her. She was awfully quiet. He turned swiftly on the bed, forcing himself to confront whatever damage he might have done.

Corinne lay very still. She had pulled the sheet up almost to her chin, and she appeared pale and faintly forlorn against the blue, flower-sprigged sheet. His heart lurched with a feeling of tenderness so intense that it was physically painful. Dear God, he would never forgive himself if he had ruined her first experience of lovemaking.

He reached out and smoothed a strand of silvery-gold hair away from her face. "Corinne," he said huskily, "are you all right? Did I hurt you very much?"

"You didn't hurt me at all."

"But you cried out when I—entered—you."

Color rose in her cheeks, tinting her fair skin a delicate shade of pink. "That wasn't from pain," she said. "At least, not exactly."

She was so beautiful to him at that moment that he wanted to take her in his arms and start making love to her all over again. He resisted the impulse. His conscience might have been operating in pretty low gear recently, but he did still have one. Lying back against the pillows, he gathered her into the crook of his arm, relieved when she curled against him without any resistance. In the process, however, the sheet she had pulled up to cover herself twisted between them. Dan wasn't sure whether to feel relief because he was at least one layer of cloth away from temptation, or regret for his deprivation. Her skin was so soft, and her slender body so inviting. He wanted to lose himself inside her again, and watch her face when he brought her to the pinnacle of pleasure.

With considerable difficulty, he managed to stop thinking about the delights of their recent lovemaking. "Corinne," he said, "we need to do some serious talking. Why didn't you tell me you were a virgin? Dammit, you're twenty-six years old, and you were married for seven years. Why in the world are you still a virgin?"

Her blue eyes darkened with a faint hint of laughter. "Times do change, don't they? Fifty years ago, a husband would have wanted to know why his bride wasn't pure, but you seem to be furious because I am. Honestly, Dan, you're reacting as though my virginity were some sort of unacceptable social disease."

"I'm reacting this way because I'm shocked. You were married for seven years, Corinne, and widows aren't usually virgins."

She moved away from him and sat up, clasping her hands around her knees. He could tell she was choosing her words very carefully. "Your uncle was a sick man all the time we were married," she said quietly. "A sexual relationship probably wouldn't have been possible, even if we'd wanted to have one."

"Are you saying Charlie was impotent?"

"We never tried to find out. I've told you before, Dan, your uncle and I didn't have a typical marriage."

"You neglected to tell me just how unusual it was."

She flinched slightly, and he cursed himself for the harshness of his tone. "Charlie's first wife died when you were still a toddler," she said. "Did you know that she died in childbirth? And that their little girl died two days later? I think Charlie thought of me more as a replacement for the daughter he'd lost than as a successor to his first wife. I know I looked up to him as the father I'd always wished I could have."

"If your relationship was so platonic, why did you get married?"

"Charlie suggested we marry because legally that was easier than going through an adoption process, particularly since my real father was still alive. Remember, at the time we were making these decisions, we thought he had a maximum of six months to live. If we'd known he was going to survive nearly seven years, we might have arranged things differently. But then again, maybe we wouldn't have. We were both very happy with the way our lives worked out."

"Seven years is a long time, Corinne. Did you ever

consider having an affair?"

"No, not really. Having a sexual relationship with another man would have seemed like a betrayal of Charlie's trust. I don't think I could have made love to somebody and still remained married to your uncle."

Dan thought briefly of Mary Beth, who had made a travesty of their marriage vows with more men than he'd ever managed to count. Oddly enough, the memory no longer brought him pain. He suddenly realized he felt sorry for his ex-wife. Her values were so shallow, she could never begin to comprehend the sort of loyalty that had kept Corinne celibate through seven years of marriage to a dying man.

The spectre of his failed first marriage did nothing to soothe Dan's nagging guilt. The truth was, he acknowledged, he had mishandled his relationship with Corinne right from the first. His experiences with Mary Beth had left him gun shy where women were concerned, and he had spent most of the past five years avoiding situations that required emotional involvement. There had never been any real need to invest time and energy in his relationships. He had found plenty of women, like Suzanne McNally, who were only too willing to share their beds without requiring anything other than a sophisticated line of sexual banter over cocktails and a slick technique once they were between the sheets.

His relationship with Corinne had been different from the very beginning, although he had no clear idea when his initial feelings of rage and suspicion had turned into something quite different.

Perhaps it had happened when he came back from Washington and found his company headquarters miraculously transformed. Perhaps it had been that day in the lunchroom when he felt his heart race as he held her in his arms. Or perhaps it started as he watched her make friends with everybody she came into contact with, from his staid, motherly secretary right down to the surly weekend janitor. Certainly, when he saw her walking toward him that morning, her wedding dress shimmering in the sunlight and the ribbons of her hat floating in the summer breeze, he knew he was in big emotional trouble. Dan shied away from any mention of the word *love*, but he had an uneasy suspicion that love was precisely what he was now feeling for Corinne.

Ironically, he knew he had no right to tell her how he felt. When he'd accepted Corinne's proposal, he had assumed she was a woman of considerable experience. Now he knew she was anything but. Somehow, agreeing to impregnate an experienced woman seemed very different from making the same agreement with a woman who was sexually unawakened—a virgin, for heaven's sake! He hadn't known the species still existed outside of high schools and convents. Chronologically, Corinne was twenty-six-years old, but in terms of experience she was a child who had never been given the opportunity to fall genuinely in love.

He had been Mary Beth's first lover, and he still felt a lingering guilt because he hadn't helped her untangle her feelings for him as a person from her feelings for him as the man responsible for her sexual initiation. He and Mary Beth had both paid dearly for his omission. This time, he owed it to Corinne, and to himself, to behave more maturely.

If he became the father of Corinne's child, he suspected he wouldn't have too much difficulty persuading her to stay married. For a moment he was sorely tempted. He would sweep her into his arms, tell her he was crazy about her, and kiss her until she had no breath left to dispute him. Dan briefly savored his fantasy before cold reality intruded. What would happen to their relationship if she woke up one morning and realized just how much she had missed? What would happen if she realized one day that she'd fallen in love—with somebody else?

Corinne had rejected the possibility of falling in love, but she was too naive to know what she was doing. The fact that her parents' marriage had been so destructive shouldn't be allowed to dominate her life. If he really cared for her, Dan realized, he had an obligation to save her from making a costly mistake. There was no way he'd be able to live with his conscience if he got her pregnant before she ever had a chance to meet a man she could really love.

He scowled. If he followed his instincts, he knew he would simply haul Corinne into his arms and make love to her until she had no energy left even to think about another man. Unfortunately, his code of honor demanded that he shouldn't give way to those instincts. He eased himself up in the bed, pulling the blanket over him as casually as he could. As soon as his body was safely armored, he turned toward Corinne. She looked more damn beautiful every time he saw her.

Dan dragged his fingers through his hair, then folded his arms across his chest. That way there was at least a passing chance he might manage to keep his hands off her delectable body.

"Look, Corinne, we have to be realistic about this situation," he said curtly. "The truth is, I'd never have agreed to your proposition if I'd known you were a virgin. I always thought the idea was more than a little crazy. Now I know it was totally insane."

"What has my virginity got to do with anything, for heaven's sake? Besides, I'm not a virgin anymore. If that ever was a problem, you've just taken care of it."

Dan winced. "You may not be a virgin anymore, but you're still a totally inexperienced woman. Corinne, believe me, you haven't explored enough options yet to know what you really want to do with your life. You've jumped from a non-marriage with Charlie straight into an attempt at instant motherhood without checking out any of the other opportunities in between. You've never given yourself a chance to develop a real, honest relationship with a man you could love."

"You're confusing sexual experience with emotional maturity. I'm not mentally deficient just because I haven't been to bed with a dozen different men." There was a tiny pause. "I'm sorry if you didn't find me a very interesting lover. I'm sure I'll get better as we go along."

Hearing the tremor in her voice, he reached out automatically to comfort her—and recovered himself just in time. If he wasn't very careful, they were going to end up stretched out on the bed making love again.

"I'm not recommending that you take on a string of lovers," he said tersely. "I'm just recommending that you wait a while longer before plunging into parenthood with a man you don't care about as the father.

"But I know exactly what I want," Corinne said. "I want to have a child, and I want you to be the father."

He noticed that she didn't deny she was indifferent to him. "That's only half the problem," he snapped.

"Dan," she said softly. "Please believe me—I'm not interested in falling in love. I've planned my future very carefully, and there's no room in it for falling in love."

"That sort of statement merely proves my point. If you knew what it feels like to be in love, you wouldn't dismiss the possibility so easily."

"How would you know? I distinctly remember that

when we first discussed my proposal, you said you had no idea what people mean when they talk about falling in love."

Dan cursed the accuracy of her recall. "Did I?" he said, doing his best to appear unfazed. "Then I'm sorry. But I didn't necessarily tell you the complete truth about myself, Corinne. There was no reason to do so—then."

He got up from the bed and walked into the bathroom, where he had left his robe. He put it on, tying it tightly around the waist. His mother always said that doing the right thing left a man feeling good, but he was rapidly discovering she was dead wrong. He knew he was doing the right and honorable thing where Corinne was concerned, and yet he felt totally, completely, one hundred percent lousy.

He stood by the window, staring into the darkness. "Anyway," he said, "my opinions on falling in love are beside the point right now. I think we can both see that we've made a terrible mistake, and we'd better clear it up as quickly as possible. I'm going to call Frank Goldberg tomorrow and find out how we can get a quickie divorce in Reno. I think that would be the best solution for both of us."

"Don't include me in your sweeping generalizations. A divorce definitely wouldn't be best for me." She gave a small, hurt laugh. "Tell me, Dan, did you ever intend to abide by the terms of our agreement, or did you intend all along simply to acquire my shares and then dump me? That contract Frank drew up didn't make any mention of how long we had to stay married in order for the share transaction to be valid. Was that the reason for the million-dollar payment you made me? A tiny sop thrown out for your conscience, maybe?"

Dan swore long and hard under his breath. He swung around, unable to remember when he had last felt so blazingly angry. "For your information, I didn't mention the shares because I'd forgotten all about the damn things."

"Of course," she said with quiet irony. "You married me strictly to acquire them, but in the heat of the moment you totally forgot about their existence. Forgive me if I find that a bit difficult to believe."

"Do you?" he said. "Then I'd say that's just one more symptom of your naiveté, Corinne. There are a couple of things bothering me right now, but the Dansted Corporation sure as hell isn't one of them."

"Maybe you're bothered about the other prenuptial contract we signed." She smiled tightly. "Don't waste your time worrying about whether it will stand up in court, Dan. I'm not planning to put it to the test. If you choose to renege on our bargain, you'll be home free."

It was bad enough that he was being noble and feeling lousy about it, but the fact that Corinne didn't appreciate his nobility was far worse. Her assumptions hurt his pride and left his emotions raw. He was almost overwhelmed by an intense, irrational desire to drag her down on the bed and silence her cutting remarks with a session of lovemaking that would leave her drained, exhausted, sated—and begging for more.

"We'll talk about the shares tomorrow," he said, walking quickly to the door. He picked up her robe and tossed it angrily toward the bed, the mere sight of her naked body almost enough to frustrate all his good intentions. "Here, put this on. You'll catch cold if you're not careful."

She put on the robe, then stood up beside the bed. Her eyes were mysterious dark pools that forbade him to probe her thoughts.

"Where are you going?" she asked.

"To bed," he said, knowing that he sounded brusque but unable to do a thing about it. "I'll sleep in the other room. Good night, Corinne."

Corinne had always prided herself on the fact that, unlike her mother, she was strong enough to face up to reality. The decisions she had made in the past hadn't always been correct, but they'd always evolved out of careful thought and clear-sighted evaluation of her own motives.

As the hours of sleepless night crawled slowly toward morning, however, she realized that for the past few weeks she had been systematically deceiving herself. From the moment she first met Dan, she had refused to examine her own feelings too closely for fear of what she might uncover. The truth was that the prospect of committing herself to a long-term relationship scared her, so she had carefully ignored all the evidence that suggested she was falling in love.

Making love to Dan had blown away her comforting veil of self-deception and forced her to examine her feelings honestly. By the time the sun came up, she had reached the painful conclusion that she was hopelessly and irredeemably in love. If Charlie had been the father figure she had always dreamed of, Dan was the personification of her ideal husband: strong enough to admit it when he was wrong; confident enough to show his tenderness; a lover capable of transporting her to the ultimate heights. Despite the fact that she was still scared by the prospect of committing herself to marriage, she knew she wanted to share the rest of her life with him. Which, she reflected wryly, left her with no real problems to tackle except the minor one of preventing him from calling Frank Goldberg and arranging an immediate divorce.

She tossed the covers to one side and walked thought-fully into the bathroom. She had at least a couple of things working in her favor, she decided, and she intended to utilize both of them to the full. First was the fact that Dan treated the prospect of fatherhood very seriously. Secondly, she was pretty sure he found her physically desirable. She might be sexually inexperienced, but she was nobody's fool. She had read all the same books and seen all the same movies as any other twenty-six-year-old woman, and she was fairly confident that Dan had found their lovemaking intensely fulfilling. He might feel nothing for her other than physical desire, but that at least was something to build on.

She put on her bikini and pulled a pair of shorts over it, not bothering to add a T-shirt. She spent some time with her makeup. When she finally peered into the bed-room mirror, she decided that the blush and eyeliner had succeeded in covering up most of the consequences of a sleepless night.

The kitchen was well-organized, and she soon found where Brent kept the coffee beans and percolator. She had barely started frying bacon when Dan appeared in the kitchen doorway. His hair was still damp from the shower and he was freshly shaven, but the hollows under his eyes gave him away. He hadn't slept any better than she had, Corinne thought with secret satisfaction. At least the decision to end their marriage wasn't one he was taking easily.

"That bacon smells good," he said, a touch of hesitation in his voice. "May I join you?"

She smiled as brightly as if he was an honored house guest rather than an estranged, one-day-old husband. "Sure," she said. "Do you like scrambled eggs as well?"

"Sounds wonderful," he said. "Can I help with anything?"

"You could find some napkins, maybe. Everything else is already on the table outside. It's such a hot morning, I thought we would eat on the porch."

They managed to limit their conversation to strictly neutral topics until breakfast was over, but then Dan leaned back in his chair and regarded her speculatively. "Do you have any special plans for today?"

"I plan to swim and work on my tan," she said. "How about you?"

He scrunched his napkin up into a tight ball. "I probably ought to make a few phone calls," he said.

"I see. Including one to Frank?"

"I was thinking about it."

"Dan, there's something you ought to think about before you place your call. She laced her fingers tightly together. "I might already be pregnant."

He looked up sharply. "That's a little unlikely, isn't it? Pregnancies don't usually result from one act of sexual intercourse."

"Try telling that to a high-school guidance counselor," Corinne said dryly.

He poured himself another cup of coffee and drank it quickly, not seeming to notice that it was already cold. "Was last night a likely time for you to conceive?"

"Yes, I'm afraid it was."

"I never considered the possibility that you might already be pregnant," he said curtly.

"But it's a possibility we need to consider."

"Yes, I guess it is. What do you want me to do?"

"I would prefer that you not call the lawyers until we find out whether or not I'm expecting a baby. If I am, I would like to stay married until it's born."

"How long will it be before you can be certain one way or the other?"

"If I'm not pregnant, we could know in as little as ten days."

"But if you are pregnant?"

Corinne kept her voice as calm and businesslike as Dan's. "If my period is overdue, there are blood tests that can confirm a pregnancy as early as three weeks after conception. So you see, I'm not making any heavy demands on your time."

Dan got to his feet, gathering up their plates and carrying them into the kitchen. She followed with the empty coffeepot and a bowl of fresh fruit. "I think you misunderstood me last night," he said. "I want this divorce to come through quickly for your sake, not for mine." He ran the hot water over the dishes, then abruptly shut it off and swung around to face her. "All the things I said to you last night still hold true, you know. If we continue living together, we can't do anything to make a pregnancy more likely."

She had no intention of openly disagreeing with him. For the time being it was enough that she still had three weeks to share with him. "Whatever you think best, Dan," she said meekly.

She unfastened the button at the waist of her shorts and slowly lowered the zipper. The air between them was suddenly alive with electricity.

She stepped out of her shorts. "I'm going to take a swim," she said innocently. "Want to join me?"

He looked at her, swallowed hard, then stared determinedly at a point somewhere to the right of her. "I'm already wearing my swimsuit," he said thickly.

She tossed her shorts onto the kitchen floor and made a totally unnecessary adjustment to the front clasp of her bikini top. Dan's eyes blazed hungrily as he watched her actions; then he blinked and carefully returned his gaze to the wall.

Corinne smiled. "Race you to the beach," she said, and dashed for the back door.

Chapter Eleven

CORINNE TOOK THE two strip steaks out of the refrigerator and carried them out to the backyard. "Are you ready for these?"

Dan lifted the cover of the barbecue, where two foil-wrapped potatoes were already baking, and examined the glowing coals with exaggerated care.

"I'm ready," he announced. "In the opinion of your master chef, the temperature is now perfect for broiling steaks."

"Are you by any chance the same master chef who got carried away watching the baseball game yesterday and totally destroyed our dinner?" Corinne asked.

Dan grinned, showing no sign of contrition. "The very same. But seeing as how you got to eat out at Bass River's fanciest restaurant, I don't know why you're complaining."

She made a face at him, then handed over the steaks, which he arranged carefully on the grill, shaking seasonings over them with carefree abandon. He closed the lid, dusted his fingers on the seat of his cut-off jeans, and strolled over to sit in the chair next to Corinne's.

"The air's finally cooling off a bit," he said, leaning back and staring up at the darkening sky. "It must have been at least ninety today."

"I guess it was." Corinne flapped a paper plate to scare away a moth. "We've been lucky with the weather."

"Yes, we have." There was a little pause. "Have you finished your packing?" he asked finally. "We ought to leave reasonably early tomorrow. The weatherman predicted afternoon thunderstorms, and there's no reason to drive home in pouring rain."

"I'm pretty well set," she said. She lowered her lashes and shot him a provocative glance. "In fact, I did all of our laundry this afternoon while you were sleeping in the hammock."

Dan rose to his feet, his eyes gleaming with silent laughter. "Somehow, I get the feeling that this would be a wise moment for me to check the steaks," he said.

"Ah! A man of *deep* perception."

He chuckled as he picked up the cooking tongs, and a wave of fierce, purely sexual longing swept through her. She grimaced wryly. You were in pretty bad shape when your heart started fluttering because of the sexy way a man handled the barbecue implements.

She dragged her gaze away from his bronzed forearms and watched a bird dig around in the grass, searching for a late-night snack. In many ways the past week had been thoroughly enjoyable. She and Dan had slipped into a shared routine with amazing ease. They had sailed together, swum together, relaxed on the beach, wiled away lazy afternoons reading on the patio, and eaten dinner in some of Cape Cod's most attractive restaurants. She had been startled by the way they seemed to understand each other's moods with the instinctive sensitivity of a long-married couple.

Unfortunately, their closeness had stopped short of the bedroom door. Each night, Dan had waited courteously until she went to bed before following her upstairs and retiring to sleep in the other room. Corinne was no longer as certain as she had been that he found her sexually desirable. Surely if he felt even a tenth as frustrated as she did, he would have given some indication by now.

The sound of Dan closing the grill cover jolted her out of her reverie. "Five more minutes and we can eat," he said. "I'm going to get myself a beer. Would you like one? Or maybe a glass of wine?"

"No, thanks. I still have some iced tea." She reached under her chair and held up the half-full glass.

He brought out his beer, then remained by the grill to coat the steaks with barbecue sauce. A few minutes later he carried a heaping plate across to Corinne and set it on her lap with a flourish.

"I hope you recognize perfection when you see it," he said with mock seriousness. "I told you I was a master of the barbecue coals, and tonight's dinner proves it."

"It certainly does." Corinne sniffed appreciatively, then bit into her butter-drenched corn. "Mmm . . . A few more meals like this and I'll even stop reminding you who did all the laundry this afternoon."

Dan pulled his chair closer to hers and took a swig of beer. "Boy, I was thirsty," he said as he cut into his steak. "I've noticed that you almost never drink alcohol," he remarked casually. "Any special reason?"

"I'm not wild about the taste. I can take it or leave it." She ate a few mouthfuls of baked potato, then put down her fork, feeling a sudden urge to tell Dan the truth. "My parents both drank like fishes," she said. "My dad could control his drinking to a certain extent, but my mother was a true alcoholic. The last six months of her life, I doubt she was ever completely sober. She was only thirty-six when she died of cirrhosis of the liver."

"Are you afraid of following in her footsteps?" he

asked softly. "I don't think you should be."

"No, not anymore, although I used to be terrified that one day I'd wake up, start drinking, and never be able to stop. I think that's why I went to work in a bar. I had to prove to myself that I could be around alcohol without needing to drink. Every night, as soon as I arrived at work, I would buy myself a beer. I'd drink a third of the glass, then pour the rest away. Every time I watched that beer gushing into the sink, it was a sort of victory for me. Nowadays, I'll occasionally drink a glass of wine with dinner, but usually I don't even bother. It's a tremendous relief to realize how unimportant alcohol is to me."

Dan put down his plate and leaned across to take her hand. "Corinne," he said, "I do 1—"

She held her breath. "Yes?"

"Nothing. I just wanted you to know that I think you're a very special woman. I've really enjoyed the time we've spent together this week."

She forced her voice to sound light. "It's been fun, hasn't it?"

"Yes." He stared across the shadowed garden, his profile suddenly hard in the gathering darkness. "Mary Beth and I went to Paris for our honeymoon," he said.

She chewed on a piece of meat that seemed determined to stick in her throat. "That must have been a wonderful place for a honeymoon," she said eventually.

"Any place can be wonderful if you're with the right person." Dan carefully wiped his fingers on a paper napkin. "I guess Mary Beth and I were still young enough not to notice that the only time we ever really enjoyed each other's company was when we were in bed."

At that moment, Corinne felt that bed would be a terrific place to be enjoying Dan's company. She rose swiftly to her feet, not anxious to pursue a conversation about Mary Beth's skills as a lover. "I'll take the plates inside if you're done."

He followed her into the kitchen, carrying a tray piled high with odds and ends they had needed for the barbecue. "Let's go for a walk along the beach," he said. "I could use some exercise to work off all that steak and stuff."

Corinne put the last dirty dish into the sink and dried her hands. "All right," she agreed. They strolled in silence across the grass to the fence that marked the entrance to the beach. Slipping off their sneakers, they both stepped onto the cool, slightly damp sand.

Corinne walked down to the water's edge and let the waves lap around her ankles. The sea was still warm with the aftermath of the day's sunshine, and she waded out, not stopping until some of the biggest waves were buffeting her thighs.

"Hey, it's dangerous to go too far out at night." Dan's voice was low and soft in her ear. "There are ghoulies and ghosties, not to mention a deceptive undertow."

She didn't look around. "I won't go any farther."

A wave, more powerful than any that had gone before, crested almost at the level of her waist and, for an instant, she lost her balance. Before she could steady herself, Dan's arms locked around her, pulling her tightly against his body. She closed her eyes, feeling the heat of his hands on the sea-cooled skin of her stomach, and hearing his breath rasp erratically in her ear.

Another wave crashed against her legs, pushing them inexorably closer. His hands slowly moved up from her waist to cup her breasts, and her nipples hardened at his touch. She twisted around, putting her hands behind his head and forcing his mouth down to her own.

His kiss was hungry, his tongue searching, his hands commanding. Spray from the ocean had splashed both their faces, leaving salt on his skin. She parted her lips eagerly, drinking in the taste of him.

"Oh God," he said thickly, when he lifted his mouth briefly from hers. "You're so soft, and so damn tempting. You fit so perfectly in my arms. Do you know what you've been doing to me all week?"

"The same things you've been doing to me, I hope." She tilted her head back, and he clutched her hair as his mouth plundered the creamy expanse of her throat. He kissed his way back up her neck and reclaimed her mouth with a deep, urgent thrust of his tongue.

Corinne's legs had long since lost the power to support her, so that when the next wave came, she was an easy victim. It literally swept her off her feet, and only Dan's quick action prevented her from being dragged under the water. As it was, the spray flew up in her face, and she swallowed two or three mouthfuls of salty foam before she managed to close her mouth and stop gasping for air.

Dan half-carried, half-pulled her out of the water and onto the sand. "Are you okay?" he asked, setting her on her feet and smoothing her hair out of her eyes. "Do you feel sick from the salt?"

"I'm fine. Really." Or at least, she would be fine if he would only take her back into his arms.

Dan's face was pale in the moonlight. "I can't believe I was crazy enough to stand in the middle of Nantucket Sound kissing you! And at night, no less! We're lucky we both didn't drown."

Corinne shivered as the wind from the sea struck her clammy shorts and T-shirt, and Dan rubbed her arms briskly. "We'd better get back to the house," he said.

"You need a hot shower."

There were lots of other things she needed more, but Dan had apparently lost interest in all of them. He seemed to have turned from lover to male nurse in the blink of an eye. Once they were back at the cottage, he insisted that she take a hot shower while he cleaned up the kitchen. Her suggestion that they shower together was met with a curt refusal followed by stony silence.

She came straight downstairs as soon as she was clean and dry, but Dan simply welcomed her with a friendly smile and then murmured an excuse about going upstairs to take a shower himself. After his earlier rebuff, she was too insecure to risk another. "You did a great job with the kitchen," she said, looking around the sparkling counters and resisting the impulse to burst into tears.

"At last you're beginning to realize that I'm not just another pretty face," he said teasingly.

Wondering just when his smile had acquired the power to dissolve her bones, she hung onto the kitchen counter for support and listened to him bound energetically up the stairs.

That was the last she saw of him for the night. "I think I'll go to bed as soon as I've taken my shower," he called back to her, poking his head over the bannister. "I have a book I'd like to finish before we leave tomorrow morning. So I guess I'll say good night, Corinne."

"Good night," she said, walking over to the fridge and pouring herself a glass of milk that she didn't want. She listened for a few minutes to the pounding of Dan's shower, then stalked into the living room and flipped on the television. Why was he being so stubborn? she wondered. He wanted to make love to her, she was sure of it, so why was he refusing to give way to his instincts?

Not for the first time, she wished she understood the

labyrinthine workings of the male mind. Dan's thought
processes since their wedding night had been utterly in-
comprehensible to her. However, one thing she was sure
of: before she gave up on their marriage, she was going
to lure Dan Matthews into bed with her at least once
more.

It was raining when they arrived back at Dan's apartment on Sunday afternoon, and it rained solidly for the
next three days. On the fourth day, it stopped raining
and Corinne woke up to find that her period had started.
She locked herself in the bathroom and cried for half an
hour, then washed her face in cold water, applied lots of
makeup, and ordered herself to start thinking instead of
emoting.

When she finally emerged from her room, Dan greeted
her with a hurried glance at his watch. "We're late, and
I have an important meeting scheduled for nine o'clock,"
he said. "Could you skip breakfast and get something at
the office?"

"I'll grab a cup of coffee and take it in the car. That's
all I want anyway."

They were rushing so much that they hardly spoke
until Dan eased the Mazda into the stream of traffic
speeding along the highway. When they stopped at a
traffic light, he turned and looked at her apologetically.
"Corinne, I'm sorry about this, but I had a phone call
while you were in the shower this morning, and I'm
going to have to make another quick trip to Mexico. The
local government authorities insist on having a personal
meeting with me before the joint-venture agreement is
finalized."

Corinne's stomach lurched with mingled relief and
guilt. If Dan left immediately and was out of the country

for the next few days, she wouldn't have to say anything about . . . Her thought trailed off, but her cheeks flamed with guilty heat. She wasn't in the habit of lying, even by omission.

She stared out the car window, hoping he wouldn't notice her red cheeks. "When are you planning to leave?" she asked politely.

"Mrs. Diaz's lawyers are getting panicky, and they're insisting that I leave today. I pointed out that the weekend's coming up and no Mexican officials ever work on a weekend, but they keep saying we have a lot to go over before we present our case."

"Don't worry about it, Dan. When do you think you'll be back? Next Tuesday, maybe?"

"I should be back before then, but I've worked with local government officials all over the world, and they're a breed apart. The mayor is worried that I may be planning to cut the size of the factory work force, and it could take days before they're satisfied that I've signed all the necessary papers guaranteeing jobs."

Corinne stared down at her hands. The honorable thing would be to tell Dan right now that she wasn't pregnant, in which case he would fly off to Mexico and probably expect her to be out of his apartment by the time he came back. Or she could behave dishonorably and say nothing at all. In which case, by the time he returned it would be almost three weeks since their wedding night, long enough for her to have had a positive pregnancy test. If she pretended she was already pregnant, there would be no reason for him to stay out of her bed . . .

She was scarcely conscious of making the decision. "I'm sorry you'll be gone for so long," she said, not meeting his eyes. "But have a good trip. I hope everything works out to your satisfaction."

"I'm sure it will. This is just one of those nuisance things, not a serious threat to our plans."

"What about your suitcase? You didn't have a chance to pack anything, did you?" She couldn't believe how normal and virtuous she could sound while behaving so badly.

"I keep one on standby at the office," he said. "These unexpected trips have come up before, and I've learned to be prepared. I'll get Alma to drive me to the airport, and then you'll have this car to drive home in."

"Fine."

He parked in a space close to the factory entrance, then turned in his seat. He cleared his throat and jiggled the car keys for a minute or so. "Corinne, is there— um—is there any news about whether or not you're pregnant?"

She breathed deeply and discovered that it was really amazingly easy to lie when your whole future depended on it. "I'm afraid not," she said. "But don't worry about a thing, Dan. By the time you get back from Mexico, I expect the whole problem will be over. I mean, as you pointed out, it's very unlikely that I'm pregnant."

"Yes, I suppose you're right. But it's been eleven days now, and I had hoped—"

"Oh look! There's Alma," Corinne said brightly. "Sorry to run, Dan, but I need to speak to her urgently."

Dan's return flight from Mexico landed at Logan on Friday of the following week, and Corinne met him at the airport.

He stood stock still when he saw her waiting for him at the arrivals gate, and for a fleeting instant she saw desire burn hard and bright in his eyes. He recovered himself almost immediately, however, and walked briskly toward her, leaving a good six inches between them when he stopped to greet her. To the casual observer his smile probably appeared no more than friendly, but Corinne had learned to read the subtle signs that hinted at his true feelings, and she saw the infinitesimal tightening of his jaw, the telltale flicker of a muscle in his cheek. He was nowhere near as unmoved as he seemed. He wanted to take her in his arms and kiss her, she was almost sure of it.

The knowledge gave her the courage to carry on with her plan. "Your tan is suspiciously glowing," she said, reaching up and giving him a quick kiss. She smiled casually, careful to keep the mood light. "All those telexes you sent must have been just a smokescreen. I think you've been spending more time frolicking on sunny beaches than negotiating in gloomy government offices."

"Don't I wish!" he murmured. He gazed at her searchingly. "You're looking a bit tired, Corinne. What have you been up to while my back's been turned? I'm almost afraid to walk into my office; you haven't redecorated it in pink and purple polka dots, have you?"

"Relax. I promise your office is still sober white with boring brown furniture. If I look tired, it's probably because Alma and I took the day off yesterday. We went to the amusement park with her grandchildren, and it's going to take me at least a week to recover. Have you ever escorted two sets of twins on a roller coaster? Or watched four little mouths stuff themselves with corn dogs, popcorn, and fudge-ripple ice cream all at the same time?"

He grinned. "No, thank God. My sisters both had the good sense to produce their children one at a time, and Alma's never invited me to share the bliss of a day with her brood."

He stepped onto the moving walkway, then turned to help her up. He neglected to let go of her hand, and his attempt to sound casual wasn't entirely successful. "I take it we no longer have to worry about the fact that you might be pregnant?"

Corinne waited for a few seconds before answering him. "I'm sorry, Dan," she murmured. "Nothing is certain yet. I had a test this morning at the doctor's office, and the results will come through this afternoon. I'm going there as soon as I've driven you back to the office."

Her words were superficially true. The doctor had, in fact, discovered that she was suffering from a minor iron deficiency and had called her into the office for a routine blood count. But Corinne knew that by implication she was blatantly lying. Dan could not help but put an entirely false construction on her words.

His face paled beneath his tan. "How likely is it that you're pregnant?"

"The doctor hasn't given me an opinion." Naturally not, since he hadn't been asked for one. Corinne stepped off the walkway, watching her feet so that she had an excuse not to look at Dan. "We'll just have to wait for the test results," she said. "It's the only way to be sure."

She dropped Dan off, then drove to the doctor's office. His nurse informed her that her blood count was now normal, but that she should continue taking an iron supplement for another month. Corinne headed back to the apartment, stopping at the supermarket on the way. Fortunately, she was too busy planning her tactics for the upcoming evening to feel as guilty as she knew she should.

After letting herself into the silent apartment, she unpacked the groceries and prepared a simple dinner of chicken breasts in wine and a marinated mushroom salad, neither of which required much last-minute attention. She set the table with the linen, china, and crystal she and Dan had been given as wedding presents, decorating the center with tall pink candles and a bouquet of carnations.

At five o'clock she ran a bubble bath, but she had scarcely immersed herself in the foam before she decided to abandon her plans for a long, leisurely soak. Lying idly in warm water gave her conscience too great an opportunity to spring into action. She let out the bath water, toweled off hurriedly, and wrapped herself in an old bathrobe. She practiced looking sultry in front of the bedroom mirror, but the results were discouraging, even when she substituted her midnight blue satin lounging pajamas for the old robe. Dreaming up a grand seduction was all very well in theory. In reality, she was afraid she lacked some of the essential equipment.

Corinne sat down on the bed and wondered what on earth she could do to occupy herself until Dan came home. He never left the office before six-thirty, which meant she had more than two hours to fill. Even if she spent an hour combing her hair and putting on makeup— an almost unimaginable feat—she would still be left with an empty hour.

In the end, she decided to bake a cake. She unearthed a recipe book and set about making a triple-layer chocolate confection that was complicated enough to require her complete attention. She was just beating the requisite three eggs when she heard the sound of Dan's footsteps marching down the hallway. The footsteps halted as he paused in the kitchen doorway. The late afternoon sun burnished the golden highlights in his thick brown hair. He carried his jacket slung carelessly over one shoulder. His dark trousers clung to his hips, and his starched white shirt seemed molded to his broad chest.

As they stared at each other for a long, silent moment, she felt herself go weak with longing. The wire wisk dropped from her fingers and clattered onto the counter. She picked it up and went to the sink, rinsing her hands and giving herself time to regain her control.

"You're home early," she said, reaching for a towel.

"I hitched a ride with Warren. He was coming in this direction."

"I wasn't expecting you for another two hours."

"I couldn't wait any longer. I needed to know." He strode across the kitchen, seized her without warning and twisted her around to face him. The towel fell unheeded to the floor. "What did the doctor say?" he demanded. "Are you pregnant?"

Corinne stared at the knot of his tie. "The test was positive," she said huskily.

For a moment, his body went rigid, and the pressure of his arms tightened. Then his hold gentled, and he hugged her against his chest, tenderly stroking her hair. "Oh *hell,* Corinne! I'm so sorry."

"Don't be sorry, at least not for me. I want to have your child, Dan." She pulled herself a little way out of his arms and looked up at him soberly. "Please answer me honestly. Do you mind very much? For yourself, I mean, not for me."

He was silent for a second or so before answering her. "No, I don't mind for myself. I'm thirty-three years old, and I decided before I ever accepted your proposal that I was ready to have a child."

"Then neither of us has any cause for regret," she said softly.

He rocked her gently for a few minutes, and she nestled her cheek against the starched front of his shirt. When she looked up, she saw that his eyes had grown heavy-lidded with desire. "Make love to me, Dan," she whispered. "Please."

His cheeks flushed darkly. "I suppose it can't make any difference now," he said, his voice husky. "God knows, I'm nearly insane with wanting you."

"I want you, too." Her hands were trembling as she reached for the sash that fastened her jacket. She untied the knot and pushed apart the lapels, allowing the jacket to slip off her shoulders and slide slowly down her body. Dan exhaled sharply when he realized that she was naked beneath the soft material.

He pulled her back into his arms, running his fingers over her narrow waist and slipping inside the satin trousers to caress her flat, firm stomach. "Your body hasn't changed yet," he said wonderingly. "But in a few weeks I'll be able to feel my child growing here, inside of you."

His hand traveled slowly up her torso and closed around her breast. She arched immediately to his touch, melting against him, parting her lips hungrily to receive his kiss.

He kissed her repeatedly, each kiss more passionate than the one before, and she responded with all the pent-up longing of three lonely, frustrating weeks. She raked her fingers through his hair, gasping when he bent her over his arm and closed his mouth around one aching nipple.

"Do you like that?" he whispered fiercely.

"Yes." Her voice was a breathless murmur deep in her throat. She held his head against her breast. "Don't stop, Dan. Please don't stop."

"I don't intend to," he said, swinging her up in his arms and carrying her into the bedroom.

They sank together onto the bed, and her fingers fumbled with the buttons of his shirt. He pulled himself out of her arms, ripping impatiently at his clothes, flinging them onto the floor and rejoining her as quickly as he could. His mouth reclaimed possession of her lips, and he cupped her breast with sure, confident fingers. His other hand brushed down her body, pausing briefly to remove the satin trousers, then feathering swiftly between her thighs.

Within seconds, she was ready for him, but he ignored the frantic quivering of her body, bringing her time and again to the brink and then denying her the ultimate release she craved. She clutched at him, beyond pride, begging for release, crying out his name when he finally entered her. But still he refused her satisfaction, holding her hips so that she couldn't speed the pace of his movements, kissing her until she was mindless with longing.

He lifted his mouth just enough for her to hear his voice. "Last time I was too quick for you," he said. Only the sweat beading on his forehead indicated how much his control was costing him. "This time we'll wait until you're ready."

If they waited any longer, she would die of ecstasy. She shuddered beneath him, feeling her nails claw at his back but unable to control her own actions.

"Dan, please, I'm ready," she panted, and he insinuated his hands beneath her hips, raising her up to receive his final, climactic thrusts.

"Come with me, sweetheart," he said in a hoarse whisper. "I want us to be there together."

Beyond coherent speech, she couldn't answer him. Her cry of pleasure choked off abruptly and her body convulsed, matching his groan of passion with the trembling heat of her own silent ecstasy.

Chapter Twelve

DURING THAT LONG NIGHT, Dan taught her more about her body than she had learned in all of the previous twenty-six years. He showed her that lovemaking could be sweet and slow, or hot and urgent, but for Corinne the result was always the same: eventually her body would collapse in his arms, quivering in joyous, abandoned release.

Dawn lightened the sky while she was still in his arms. The first fingers of sunlight crept into the bedroom, illuminating the shadowy corners and warming her sensitized skin. Dan lay sprawled on the bed, his arm stretched across her stomach in a gesture of lazy possession. He rolled over, propped himself on one elbow, and gently tickled the underside of her breasts.

She smiled sleepily, not opening her eyes. "I think that feels good, but I'm too exhausted to decide."

His fingers swept in a series of slow circles around her abdomen. "Corinne," he said quietly, "it was good for both of us tonight, wasn't it?"

She was drifting closer and closer to sleep. "Mmm..."

"And we had fun together when we were in Cape Cod."

"Mmm..."

"And we work well together, now that we're not ar-

177

guing about the company shares."

"Mmm..."

"Well then, how would you feel if we forgot all about our prenuptial contracts and tried to make this marriage into something real and permanent? Personally, I think it's worth a shot. Our child would do much better growing up in a home with two parents, don't you think?"

She was instantly wide awake. She sat up in bed, edging away from him, needing some physical distance between them so she could at least try to think. She pushed her tumbled hair out of her eyes. "You mean— you want us to stay married to each other for the sake of the baby?"

"Yes. Why not? There are worse reasons for staying together, and I reckon that he, or she, deserves a chance at a normal two-parent family."

Corinne didn't answer him at once. She noticed a pillow lying on the floor, tossed there in some earlier moment of blind passion. She picked it up and hugged it to her cold body. How ironic that Dan was offering her everything she wanted—but for the entirely wrong reasons. She took her courage firmly in both hands.

"There isn't going to be any baby," she said. "I lied to you, Dan. I'm not pregnant."

"You mean the test result yesterday was negative, not positive?"

"I never had a pregnancy test." She was clutching the pillow so tightly that her fingers had turned numb. "The truth is, Dan, I knew the day you left for Mexico that I wasn't expecting a baby."

His eyes probed her features. "Then why in God's name didn't you tell me?"

Pride urged her to hold back the truth, but she spoke without caution, long past the stage of attempting to conceal her feelings. "I wanted you to make love to me again," she admitted. "And I didn't think you would unless you thought I was already pregnant."

"I see." He leaned across the bed and crooked his finger under her chin, forcing her to look at him. Corinne had expected him to be absolutely furious, but she detected no hint of the explosive anger she'd anticipated.

"I'm not sure I understand you correctly," he said. "Do you mean you still haven't given up on your crazy scheme to get pregnant by some man you don't care about? Is that why you wanted to get me back in your bed? So I could provide stud service and then obligingly pick up my Dansted Corporation shares and disappear into the mist?"

"No," she said swiftly. "I told you once that I would never trick a man into becoming a father, and I meant what I said. I saw my gynecologist while you were in Mexico, and he recommended some birth-control precautions. There's no danger of a pregnancy resulting from what happened tonight, Dan, I swear it."

He took the pillow out of her arms and threw it onto the floor. "Then would you mind answering my question, Corinne? Why were you so anxious to persuade me to make love to you again?"

Corinne's emotions welled up like an underground spring, confined too long without an outlet. "Because I love you," she said. "Because I wanted to give us some time together, so that maybe you'd decide you liked being married to me." She laughed harshly. "Isn't that a good joke, Dan? After all those claims I made about never falling in love, I fell in love with the very man Charlie had picked out for me."

"*Charlie?*"

"Yes. I think Charlie deliberately set up his will so

we'd have no choice but to be thrown together. He didn't know anything about my plans to have a baby, of course, but he figured that once we got to know each other, we wouldn't be able to keep from falling in love." She choked back a laugh that was perilously close to a sob. "Well, I guess he was at least half right."

Dan leaned forward and slowly pushed her back against the mattress. He captured her hands and held them high over her head, exposing her entire body to his gaze.

"No," he said, bending down and trailing a line of passionate kisses across her stomach. "Good old Uncle Charlie wasn't half right. He was bang on the button, as always. Oh, sweetheart, haven't you realized yet that I'm totally and hopelessly in love with you? Why do you think I invented that feeble excuse to fly back to Mexico?"

Corinne stared. "What feeble excuse?"

"Honey, the Mexican mayor and his problems could have been handled with a couple of quick telephone calls, but I had to invent some way of getting out of this apartment. By the time we came back from Bass River, all I had to do was look at you and I was on fire. I was determined to do the honorable thing and save you from a loveless marriage, but my willpower only stretches so far. After three rainy evenings sitting in the living room and imagining you in this bed, my self-control was shot to hell."

The sun climbed over the horizon, bathing the bedroom in a warm, golden light. Corinne felt light-headed with happiness. She reached up to stroke his cheek, roughened by early morning stubble. "Dan, are you telling me you love me?"

"I'd much prefer to show you," he said. "But I'll tell you if you insist. I love you, Corinne, in ways that I didn't even know were possible. I want to have you in my bed at night. I want us to have children together, and bring them up as a family. I want to know that I'm going to see you across the breakfast table every morning for the next fifty years."

She smiled. "I've been on my best behavior since we were married. If you knew what a grouch I really am first thing in the morning, you'd never make such a rash statement."

"But I want to find out all about you, even the grouchy parts." He caught her hand and held it against his face, then pressed a brief, hard kiss against her palm. "Because I love you."

Tears glimmered in her eyes, and he brushed them away with trembling fingers. His mouth seared her skin, rediscovering all the places that he alone had touched, making her wild for his possession. As she whispered his name, he took her swiftly, parting her legs and sliding into her, carrying her away on a sea of pleasure more intense than any that had gone before.

Afterward, she smiled at him dreamily, her eyes closed and her body limp in his arms. "Dan," she said, her voice a husky whisper deep in her throat. "I love y . . ."

She was already asleep when he gathered her into the crook of his arm, and he smiled tenderly as she curled trustingly against him. He pulled the sheet up over them both and slid carefully down the bed, yawning. They could afford to sleep for a few hours. After all, they had a lifetime of mornings ahead of them.

GREAT BOOKS

E-BOOKS

AUDIOBOOKS

& MORE

Visit us today

www.speakingvolumes.us

Printed in Great Britain
by Amazon